VALKYRIE HEART

VALKYRIE BOUND #1

NICHOLE ROSE

Copyright © 2024 by Nichole Rose

All rights reserved.

No portion of this book may be reproduced in any form without written permission from the publisher or author, except as permitted by U.S. copyright law.

Cover by Yoly at Cormar Covers

Contents

About the Book	1
Content Advisory	3
Prophecy of the Valkyrie	4
Glossary of Common Terms	5
Prologue	7
Chapter One	16
Chapter Two	36
Chapter Three	50
Chapter Four	62
Chapter Five	78
Chapter Six	95
Chapter Seven	122
Chapter Eight	137
Chapter Nine	159
Chapter Ten	184

Chapter Eleven	198
Chapter Twelve	205
Chapter Thirteen	213
Chapter Fourteen	215
Chapter Fifteen	226
Author's Note	230
Valkyrie Bound Series	231
A Bride for the Beast	233
Follow Nichole	236
Nichole's Book Beauties	238
Instalove Book Club	239
Also by Nichole Rose	240
About Nichole Rose	248

About the Book

FORGED IN BATTLE AND **bound by destiny, will their love become their ultimate weapon against the Dark?**

Dax

For millennia, I was oathbound to protect Valhalla, a warrior of Light sworn to defend her no matter the cost. Until the Forsaken cast the Fae out and destroyed every last Valkyrie within her borders. The Fae have been trapped on earth since, waiting for the five mortal women meant to save us all.

It's too peaceful. Too still. And I was born for war.

But when Rissa's soul calls to mine, I realize that maybe peace isn't so bad after all. If it means keeping her safe, I'll lay my weapons down in a heartbeat.

Fate has other plans.

My mate is one of the five. And the Forsaken won't stop until she's dead. I'll do whatever I have to do to protect her and our bond. Even if it means letting Valhalla fall forever.

Gods help anyone who stands in my way.

Rissa

My entire life, I've been different. I've felt things I shouldn't. Heard things that weren't there. But those whispers never led me astray until my twenty-first birthday. The handsome stranger I met at the bar seemed innocent enough...until I woke up in his bed with no recollection of how I got there.

He says I'm not who I think I am. The craziest part? The more time I spend with him, the more I want to believe it when he says he belongs to me. But my life isn't a fairytale, and a mate bond with an ancient Fae warrior isn't the start of my happily ever after.

It might just be the end of everything.

How am I supposed to stand against the Dark when I don't even know who I am?

Content Advisory

T HIS BOOK ADDRESSES DARK subject matter (including domestic violence, not between MMC and FMC) that may not be suitable for all readers.

Prophecy of the Valkyrie

"*I*N A REALM *of shadows, five shall emerge, each carrying the sacred gifts bestowed by their foremothers. As they step into the light, the echoes of time will guide their way, revealing what once was lost. The Exiled, weary and burdened, shall embark on a perilous quest to restore honor for the Halls. Yet, a cautionary whisper resonates: tread carefully in the presence of the Forsaken. If the sisters falter, a torrent of great evil will engulf the realms, casting them into an eternal night.*"

-Prophecy of the Valkyrie

Glossary of Common Terms

This book includes some words in Old Norse, Swedish, Norwegian, and Icelandic, the languages of the Nothern people whose beliefs, myths, and stories are woven throughout this series. Some of the those commonly used throughout the book can be found below.

ja - Yes/Yeah

nei – no

lyststål – lightsword

Magn – Source of Fae power. Literally, power or force.

ást-meer - sweetheart

helvete - hell

skíta - shit

faen - fuck

níðingr – insult meaning cowardly, dishonorable person

eselballer – donkey balls

ímun-laukr - sword

ljós - light

elskan-ljós - Beloved light

bittesmå ljós - tiny light
lyseste ljós - brightest
konung-ligr - royal
konunga-kyn - royal kin
helveteshundar- hellhounds
varulv – werewolf/wolf

Alt du gjør er gjort i kjærlighet – Everything you do, you do in love.

Du er i min verden – You are my world.

Hundre riker ville være for få til å inneholde min kjærlighet til deg – A hundred kingdoms aren't enough to contain my love for you.

Prologue

Dax

VALHALLA, 300 YEARS AGO

The stench of war lies heavy in the air, settling in the back of my throat. The sickly, sweet scents of blood and death mix with smoke and ash, threatening to choke every last remaining Light out of Valhalla. I grit my teeth against that grim reality and race around the edge of the Hall of Warriors, my *lyststål* blazing like a sun in my hands.

Shouts and the screams of the dying ring out around me. There are far fewer of them now than there were just an hour ago. And fewer still than there were yesterday and the day before that. None are women. Not any longer.

There's no denying the truth anymore.

The last of the Valkyrie have fallen.

An endless well of grief bubbles up from my soul, threatening to consume me. I slam a lid on it, reaching deep for anger instead. *Ja.* Anger. The furious churn of rage eating like acid through my stomach. It's what drives the Fae now. What fuels us.

Rage.

The Valkyrie have fallen. And Gods have mercy on the souls of the Forsaken who claimed their Light, for the Fae will have none for them.

"Dax! *Til venstre! Til venstre!*" Adriel's shouted warning about an enemy on the left reaches my ears just in time.

I feint to the right, my *lyststål* spinning in my hands.

It slices through the neck of an armored *varulv*, one of the shifters the Forsaken turned to the dark long ago, separating his head from his shoulders. His body drops, warm blood spraying across my face. Tendrils of smoke float from the wound my *lyststål* left, carried by the wind. I drag the back of my hand across my face, flinging off the foul blood of the soul-damned monster before turning to check on my brothers.

My breath catches in my throat.

Once, Valhalla was a place of beauty, a paradise. Now, it lies in ruin, destroyed by our Forsaken invaders and their monstrous army. The once radiant Hall of Warriors is a charred, twisted relic. Bodies litter the valley, turning the lush green fields red. The barracks have burnt to the ground, leaving nothing but smoking piles of ash.

There's nothing left to save.

We've failed.

Valhalla, like *Álfheimr*, lies in ruin.

A flash at the edge of the valley captures my attention. It's nothing more than a brief flicker, gone as soon as it appears. But I shift my gaze toward it on instinct. For a long moment, nothing moves. And then the same flicker reaches me. I release my hold on *Magn*, the source of Fae power, allowing my *lyststål* to dissolve in my hands. Without it blazing like a nimbus, I see what I didn't before.

Something unseen strikes against the portal, causing the bright surface to momentarily turn a sickly gray and let off a shower of sparks. It does it again, and then again.

Horror surges through me as realization dawns. The Forsaken are trying to bring it down!

Gods alive. If they destroy it, Valhalla won't just lie in ruin. It'll fall completely, cut off entirely from Asgard. There are no Valkyrie left alive to reopen it. Just like there are none left to usher the souls of the dead across the Veil.

Ragnarök claimed nearly every Valkyrie life, along with the souls of every warrior bonded to her, two thousand years ago. The Forsaken and their dark magic have claimed the rest.

But the Fae still stand. Some of us, at least. And so long as we stand, our oath remains unbroken. We're the guardians of Valhalla, the army of Light appointed by Odin himself to defend the Valkyrie, no matter what comes.

The portal cannot fall.

"Fae! *Beskytt portalen*!" I roar, leaping over the fallen *varulv* in a dead race across the valley toward the portal. I reach for *Magn*, my *lyststål* blazing back to life. "*Beskytt portalen!* They're trying to bring it down!"

Roars of fury echo from every corner of the valley as my brothers take up the cry. Within moments, Malachi, Adriel, and Damrion are at my side, racing across the valley with me. One Forsaken warrior after another falls to our blades, unable to stand against the Light. *Varulv*, *Jötunn*, and Forsaken alike taste death as we deal it to them, one by one.

There will be no raising their souls this time. What dies by our hands stays dead.

By the time we reach the portal, Reaper is already there, his blade spinning as he fells *Jötunn* after *Jötunn*, a savage snarl on his face.

"It's about time the four of you show up," he growls. "Thought I was going to have to kill them all myself."

"Sorry, but mamma said you have to share," Malachi rumbles with a cheeky grin, plunging his blade through the chest of an armored giant. The steel, like flesh, turns red hot, melting under the intense blast of Light. Malachi plants his foot in the dying *Jötunn's* chest, kicking him off his *lyststål*.

"Then I guess it's a good thing there are several hundred of them, isn't it?"

"You go left, I'll go right," Malachi says without missing a beat. "Our brothers can take the middle."

"*Nei*." Damrion shakes his head, halting my brothers before they can surge forward. "Whatever the Forsaken are doing to the portal, they're doing from Asgard. We need to go through."

"If the portal falls with us on the other side, we'll be cut off from Valhalla," Adriel growls.

"And if we're here when it falls, we fall with Valhalla," Damrion snaps back, his gold eyes hard. "We can't see the prophecy fulfilled if we die."

"And our brothers?" Adriel demands, refusing to back down. "You'd leave them to die in our place?"

"*Nei*. Dax already sounded the call. They're on the way."

Adriel mutters an oath, anger glittering in his eyes. He knows Damrion is right, though. If our brothers can reach us, they will. If they can't, there is no saving them, no matter what we do. They'll die where they stand, alongside every *Jötunn*, *varulv*, and Forsaken still on this side of the portal.

Gods alive. Do the *Jötunn* and *varulv* even know what's going to happen to them if the portal falls? Did the Forsaken tell them, or did they keep that secret to themselves?

"He's right, Adriel," Malachi, ever the peacekeeper between the two, says. "We need to stop whatever Gods' forsaken foul magic they're weaving on the portal."

"Gods have mercy on our souls," Adriel spits, the scar bisecting his eye giving the comment a foreboding edge.

"I could use a little help here," Reaper shouts as the *Jötunn* surge forward again, trying to drive us back into the valley.

We step forward as a unit, *lyststål* blazing. One after another after another, *Jötunn* fall beneath our blades. Malachi takes a hammer blow across the back, but it doesn't slow him much. Nothing ever does. Peacekeeper he may be, but in times of war, he's as lethal and unyielding as any Fae.

Eventually, more of the Fae reach us. By the time we make it to the portal, we're over two hundred strong. The *Jötunn* scatter like mice, fleeing in every direction from the wall of burning steel marching closer and closer.

The once bright, shining surface of the portal ripples as the Forsaken on the other side attack it with their perverse magic. Showers of sparks rain down like tears, as if the portal itself weeps for the fate awaiting Valhalla if it falls.

"*Lyststål* and shields at the ready!" Damrion orders, his voice booming over the Fae. "When we reach the other side, we kill everything in our path or die where we stand."

I grip my sword, prepared for death. I've spent the last three thousand years surrounded by it, defending Valhalla. It's an old, familiar friend. One I welcome whenever it comes.

"*Mot døden*!" Damrion shouts, lifting his sword over his head.

"*Mot døden*!" two-hundred Fae roar as one. Yes, we'll march toward death.

We advance, racing toward the portal with *lyststål* and shields at the ready.

Malachi, Damrion, and Reaper plunge through first. Adriel and I are hot on their heels. Fae after Fae pours through the portal behind us. Unlike usual, it doesn't light up. It isn't warm. There is no welcome. It's ice cold and black as midnight, corrupted by whatever magic the Forsaken have woven over it. Not even the light from my *lyststål* pierces the pervading darkness.

I gasp as icy fingers rake down my back, chilling me all the way to my soul. They pick me apart fragment by fragment before forcing me back together. It wrests *Magn* from my control, sending my *lyststål* spinning back into the elements. My shield dissolves too, leaving me empty-handed and grasping.

The strange sensation ends as quickly as it began.

I stumble out of the portal, shivering.

Light blazes all around me as my brothers reach for *Magn*, channeling their *lyststål* and shields back into their hands. I'm a split second behind, prepared to defend my brothers, Valhalla, and the portal with my dying breath.

Except there are no Forsaken here. And this isn't Asgard. There are no crumbling halls of gold, no once Shining City. Massive trees loom up on every side, plunging high into a star-filled sky. A single moon shines brightly overhead, tufts of cloud floating across an endless expanse of midnight blue. Ice crunches beneath our boots, a thick film of it covering everything.

All around me, my brothers notice the same things, heads whipping this way and that as they try to figure out where we are. I know, though. I've seen this realm often enough over the years, the one so much like *Álfheimr*.

Midgard. Earth.

The portal brought us to earth.

"*Helvete*," Malachi breathes.

"Close enough." Reaper's upper lip curls. "*Midgard.*"

"Why did the portal spit us out here?" I look to Damrion for my answer, not entirely convinced he has it, either. But he's the oldest of us, the only one with royal blood running through his veins. If anyone has a guess, he should.

He shakes his head, his lips pursed.

The portal groans behind us, a Gods-awful screeching noise that sets my teeth on edge.

I spin to face it, *lyststål* at the ready.

Chaos erupts as the portal wobbles, the rainbow surface turning pitch black. Screams sound from within as the entire thing goes up in flames that burn so hot I feel the heat of them scorching fine hairs all over my arms.

The portal groans a final time, and then collapses in upon itself with a roar.

The Fae standing closest are blown off their feet, landing in heaps as the portal fails, taking Valhalla with it...and leaving two-hundred Fae stranded on earth.

Chapter One

Dax

Seattle, Present Day

Death is a familiar friend. I've spent millennia surrounded by it, my sword and soul pledged to the protection of the Valkyrie, the Guardians of the Dead. I still can't stand the sound of silence. It's too peaceful. Too still. And I was built for war.

But the Gods-forsaken racket pumping through the bar is eight full levels above tolerable. Frankly, it's torture.

It isn't music. It wasn't created for dancing or worship. It was made for fucking.

That's basically what's happening on the wooden dance floor as I stomp around the edges in search of my brothers. Human women in revealing clothing grind against men who paw all over them, alcohol and other intoxicants seeping from their pores along with sweat and the cloying scent of cheap cologne.

I've been in this city, and others like it often over the centuries, and I still don't understand this ritual of drinking to excess in places like this. Times may change, but this ritual remains the same the world over.

It's madness.

My brothers and I could massacre everyone here in minutes, and they'd be helpless to stop us. They're too intoxicated to even recognize the danger.

Skíta.

Perhaps they do recognize it. The human world is dark and violent. They've become all too familiar with the horrors that surround them and the evil that walks amongst them. Rituals like this allow them to forget for a moment just how fragile and fleeting their lives are. Perhaps drinking themselves senseless even gives them a little glimmer of hope that it'll make sense in the end.

It won't.

Life's a bitch, and then you die. And death? Well, that's a bitch, too.

Maybe once it made sense. Once, there was a purpose to it.

That was a long time ago...before Valhalla fell. Before the dead were left to roam, their souls picked off one by one by the Forsaken.

Now? Well, like I said, death's a bitch, too.

I spot Malachi's broad shoulders rising above the crowd and veer in his direction. Even sitting at the very back of the bar as far into the shadows as he can get, he stands out like a sore thumb with his umber skin and bright blue eyes. It's an unusual combination in this world, even in an age where people change their hair and eyes as often as they do their underwear.

Then again, we all stand out, even in this age. It's hard to hide five warriors who stand head and shoulders taller than nearly every other man, woman, and child in the city. Especially five who glow if you look closely enough.

But in places like this, people rarely notice. If they do, they don't think twice about us. To most, we're simply a fragment of a memory, no more important than a piece of the room they're sitting in. The few who remember anything more than that convince themselves that we're a figment of their intoxicated minds, too unbelievable to be real.

Being immortal has its perks.

Living forever isn't one of them, but compulsion is. We can't—and won't—force the will to bend to our whim.

Only the Forsaken would dare. But we are capable of muddying the waters enough to hide our presence in this realm.

"Adaxiel." Reaper lifts amber eyes to me as I approach the table. His long hair is pulled back from his face, his distinctive ears carefully hidden within. Dressed in jeans and a T-shirt, he could almost pass as human. Almost. "Any luck?"

I shake my head, sliding onto the bench beside Adriel, who grunts before scooting over an inch to make room. "*Nei.* Nothing."

"You're sure this is the place?"

I turn a look on Adriel, who merely holds my gaze, his mangled eye covered in a patch, his good eye unflinching. "*Ja*," I say quietly. "This is the place. Abigail was certain of it."

"She could be wrong," Malachi suggests.

"Abigail is never wrong," Damrion says before I can answer. "If she says the girl will appear here; the girl will appear here. We wait."

Malachi shrugs like it makes no difference to him and goes back to nursing his beer. Adriel grimaces and leans his head back against the wall, closing his good eye. He isn't sleeping, though. Not even close. At rest, he's still one of the two most dangerous men in this room, second only to Reaper.

"What did Abigail say again?" Reaper says, curious gaze flickering between me and Damrion. His brown skin gleams under the light, his power flickering around him no matter how he masks it. His strength is the one thing he can't hide.

Luckily, those who are observant enough to notice it simply chalk it up to some inexplicable part of his beauty. They assume they're just dazzled by his looks. It's ironic, really. He's the deadliest warrior the Fae have ever known. And humans take one look at him and swoon at his feet.

He fucking hates it. Which means Malachi finds it hysterical. Naturally.

"The prophecy is in motion. The sisters have manifested. Beware, a shadow lies over Heart," Damrion and I repeat in unison. It was a hell of a Foretelling, one not easily forgotten. As soon as Abigail's eyes turned white two weeks ago, a chill went down my spine.

The human Seer—a tiny little slip of a thing who sees things before they happen—has been in Eitr, our small fortress deep in the mountains, for the last few years. She's a runaway who insists she's supposed to be there. We sent her on her way several times in the beginning, but as soon as we'd drive her back into town, she'd find her way back to Eitr.

Fully grown explorers can't even find us. But a tiny little slip of a girl found her way to us three separate times. It was enough to give us pause. We stopped trying to send her back to her foster home at all when she predicted the arrival of Stephan, a former Navy SEAL who stumbled his way into Eitr after a bear attack.

Like Abigail, he never left. There are others like them, humans who found their way to us and made Eitr home. Most are warriors or healers or those who simply don't fit neatly into the human world...those like Abigail with gifts that defy human explanation.

Valkyrie blood runs through most of their veins.

Even in death, the Valkyrie still serve, gathering the ancestors of their offspring to us. The Blooded have been coming more frequently over the last few years, as if they sense the same shift in the wind we've sensed. As if they know the time has come.

Valhalla is rising...and so are her enemies. If my brothers and I can find the five Valkyrie destined to fulfill the prophecy, we do more than simply restore Valhalla. We give the dead hope of escaping the Forsaken with their souls intact...hope they haven't had in three centuries.

We've been searching for the five Valkyrie written into the Tapestry of Time since the day we were cast out of

Valhalla. Three hundred years. Trapped in a realm that lost our memory to myth long, long ago.

"You really think she's here?" Malachi asks, his expression brooding, contemplative as he scans the bar. "In this bar?"

"Abigail believes so," Damrion says quietly. "That's enough for me."

"If she told you she shat gold, it'd be enough for you," Adriel snorts.

Damrion's face falls into a scowl.

Once, Damrion and Adriel were closer than blood brothers. And then Adriel was captured during the battle for *Álfheimr*. He spent years in captivity, tortured by the *Jötunn*. Damrion made the call not to send a rescue party, convinced the *Jötunn* wouldn't keep the captives alive after *Álfheimr* fell.

He's never forgiven himself for that decision. Neither has Adriel.

If Damrion says right, Adriel says left on principle. It's been the same way for two thousand years. The animus between them has only grown since Abigail arrived.

"Now that'd be a useful skill," Malachi says before Damrion can snap back at Adriel. "My *lyststål* has seen enough sap to last five lifetimes."

To keep up pretenses, all of the Fae take turns felling trees and clearing land around Eitr. Anyone who stumbles upon our little village leaves believing we're simple mountain folk who eke out a living on the land. The truth is far more complex than that. But we do what we must to keep humans complacent.

"Only five?" A smile ghosts across Reaper's face. "Just last week, you said seven."

"I'm not in the middle of the woods freezing my nuts off now. I'm feeling generous." Malachi grins.

Reaper's laughter booms across the table, dispelling the tension between Damrion and Adriel.

"Why here?" Adriel asks. "Of all the places she could appear, it just so happens to be Seattle?"

Reaper's laughter dries up, everyone at the table falling silent as we contemplate the question.

"The Blooded have been drawing closer to Eitr for years," Damrion finally says. "If she's one of the five, perhaps she feels the same pull to us that they have."

It's the one mercy we've been granted, though I'm not inclined to call it that. We spent centuries combing through every corner of this world in search of the five, looking for any clues to their whereabouts, waiting for their arrival. None ever came. Until Abigail. Until now.

If the portal spit us out here because this is where they were meant to appear, it begs questions I'm not sure I want to ask, let alone answer. Like whether the Forsaken were the ones who trapped us as we've always assumed, or if it was some built-in failsafe of the Gods, ensuring we had no choice but to help fulfill the prophecy. We swore our allegiance to Valhalla and the Valkyrie long ago. Best not to start questioning our choices now.

Panic surges through me out of nowhere, hitting like a bomb blast in the center of my chest. It strikes deep, slicing through every thought and every sensation, stripping me right down to the bone.

For a moment, I'm not at the table with my brothers. I'm in a dark hallway, stumbling away from a man three times my size. He leers at me, pale hands outstretched as if to grab me. My mind is fuzzy and clouded, my steps uncoordinated. My body doesn't work the way it should. But I know I don't want him to touch me. I know terror. I feel it now, clawing up my throat as realization dawns. *He drugged my drink.*

Oh, God. Please, help me.

The image winks out, leaving my field of vision black. The sense of terror doesn't go with it. That still surges through me, pumping through my veins as if it's *my* fear, *my* panic. It isn't. It's *hers*. I still feel her in my head, scared and alone.

I jump to my feet, hands raised to call *Magn* and my *lyststål* to defend her against the bastard who thinks he can take what a Valkyrie hasn't offered. I'll split him open from groin to throat, the foul, evil little *drittstøvel*.

"*Nei!*" Adriel grabs my arm. "*Nei*, Dax."

"*Slipp meg fri!*" Let me go.

"*Nei*, Dax," he says softly. "I'm not letting you go. If you channel, you'll start a panic in here."

"She's already panicking," I growl, trying to fling his arm off.

"Who?"

"My Valkyrie." I jerk out of his hold, but I don't reach for *Magn* again. The instinctive urge to kill has diminished, though it isn't gone by far. He's drugged a Valkyrie. *My* Valkyrie. Whoever he is, he'll die for that before the sun kisses the horizon. But I need to get to her first. Protect her. That's my job now. My life for hers. My soul for hers.

Ah, Gods. I need to get to her. I feel her. So scared. So helpless. Her fear beats at me. I want to howl in fury. My arms ache with the need to pull her close and protect her, to feel her in them.

"Valkyrie? You *feel* her?"

"*Ja*. She called my soul."

Every one of my brothers looks shell-shocked. I don't blame them. In all the time the Fae guarded Valhalla and the Valkyrie, not a single Valkyrie ever called the soul of a Fae. Odin forbade it. We were sworn to guard all of Valhalla, not a single Valkyrie. Had one called a Fae soul, that Fae would have let the nine realms burn to ash to protect her and her alone.

Already, I feel that need beating at me. She's mine. *Mine.*

"I guess the Old Laws no longer apply," Malachi says dryly, as if reading my mind.

They haven't applied in a long time, not since Odin and the Æsir walked the realms.

"*Faen,*" Damrion curses.

I leave them at the table to process my revelation, stalking toward the hallway to find my Valkyrie. I'll process later. After she's safe.

To their credit, my brothers are at my back within moments. We move through the bar as one. People instinctively move out of the way, parting like the seas to allow us through. A few murmur complaints. One woman makes a pass at Reaper, who simply steps around her as if she didn't speak at all.

"Prick," she shouts after him.

"Sounds like she knows you personally," Malachi whispers, ribbing him.

He grunts in response, making the mischievous warrior chuckle.

Several couples are pressed against the walls in the narrow, shadowed hallway, dry fucking as if they're in their own private chambers. I push past them, focused on finding the Valkyrie I still feel as if a current of power runs between her soul and mine.

She's close. And powerful. Gods. So powerful. Does she know who she is and what she's meant to do, or is she as clueless as every other human in this city?

Adriel and Reaper peel off to check the bathrooms while Malachi, Damrion, and I head toward the far end of the hall.

A shuffling sound reaches my ears as we near the only other door. I don't know if it's a storeroom or an exit. It isn't marked.

I kick it open anyway, hoping the Gods-forsaken music covers the noise of the splintering frame.

Cool air rushes in as the frame collapses. I catch a glimpse of a brick wall across the alley and an overflowing garbage bin.

An exit, then.

"Let me go!"

My blood boils at the sound of her voice. It's thick and uncoordinated, the words slurring together. I'm going to rip his throat out fo hurting her.

"Stop fighting and get in the car, Valkyrie."

Helvete.

Whoever has her knows what she is. How?

I call *Magn*, reaching for my *lyststål*. Power surges around me as Damrion and Reaper do the same. They heard him, too.

I step through the door, ready to end his miserable life, whoever—and whatever—he is. The desire only intensifies when he comes into view, one hand wrapped around my Valkyrie's throat as he tries to force her into the SUV idling at the head of the narrow alley. She's so tiny—so beautiful. Gods, she's perfect. Thick and curvy and gorgeous.

He isn't. Even dressed in human clothing with a baseball cap pulled down over his head, there's no hiding his pale skin or the dark shadow rippling around him.

"Forsaken," I hiss.

The Forsaken are perversions of nature, the soul-damned immortals who gave themselves over to the dark. Humans call them demons, but they don't know the half of it. The Forsaken predate any religion known to man, predate humanity. They were evil before evil had a name. The only thing they fear is the Light.

It's been three hundred years since they destroyed the portal, trapping us on earth. Three hundred years since we swore to exterminate every single one of them. And rage still roars through me in a blistering cloud.

"*Ja*, Forsaken," Damrion growls, the nimbus of light surrounding him growing brighter as he calls more power. It crackles like electricity as he hefts his *lyststål*, a savage look on his face.

"Let me go!" the Valkyrie cries again, fighting tooth and nail. She's tiny, especially in his hands. Her head barely reaches his shoulder, but she fights as fiercely as any Valkyrie. Moreso, perhaps, considering the drugs pumping through her veins.

"Silence!" The Forsaken lashes out with a whip of dark power, cutting off her air supply.

Her blue eyes go wide, her mouth open even though no sound comes out. Fear rips through me again, a fresh wave of terror crashing like a tidal wave in the center of my chest.

Rage boils over. Hers. Mine. In this moment, I'm not sure. But I'm not the only one who feels it. She does, too.

It pours out of her in an eruption of powerful Light that rivals the sun, hot, intense. *Exquisite*.

The Forsaken screams as it envelopes him, burning through him like lava. He flings himself away from her. But it's far too late for that.

He ignites like kindling, his clothing going up with a whoosh. His scream ends abruptly, cut off as her Light reduces him to ash in seconds.

"Gods have mercy," Malachi whispers into the ensuing silence.

My Valkyrie sobs, her Light winking out. Her legs wobble, threatening to drag her to the ground.

I release my *lyststål*, striding across the few feet separating us. I make it to her side just as her legs give out.

She lands in my arms, staring up at me with eyes that see clear to my soul. Even dull from the drugs in her system and the shock of what just happened here, intelligence far beyond her years blazes in her eyes. My heart slams against my ribcage, my entire system lighting up as I stare into her eyes. Gods save me. I've never seen anything more perfect. She fits in my arms precisely as if she was made to be in them. She's soft, so soft.

"Valkyrie," I whisper, my voice shaking. "*Elskan-ljós*. You're safe now."

"I..." Confusion swirls through her eyes and wrinkles her perfect brow. "Did I just kill that man?"

"*Nei, lyseste ljós*. He was no man."

"Oh." Her gaze bounces across my face. "Are you?"

"All too much," I say wryly. I've never felt more like a man than I do with her in my arms. Gods. My cock aches, my body screaming to claim what now belongs to me in a way nothing and no one will ever be able to violate or break. Now isn't the time, yet the instinctive urge to fuck and possess grows stronger the longer she's in my arms.

She's so beautiful. Dark hair frames her heart-shaped face, falling midway down her back. Plump, pink lips part slightly, the tip of her tongue dancing across them. Unlike half the women in the bar, she's dressed modestly, her thick, curvy body hidden in jeans and a hot pink top that reveals little more than a teasing glimpse of cleavage.

"Are you going to hurt me?"

"Never," I vow. I'll destroy worlds to keep her safe.

"Okay, then," she whispers. Thick, sooty lashes flutter over her eyes, her body going lax in my arms. The drugs drag her under, her strength depleted now that she knows she's safe in my arms.

"Dax."

I snarl a warning, crouching over my Valkyrie as Malachi places a hand on my shoulder. The urge to rip his hand from me is strong. The desire to take her away from him, far from everyone, is stronger. It beats at me, growing stronger the longer I ignore it.

Forsaken walk the earth. She isn't safe. It's my job to make her so.

"Easy, Dax." Malachi holds his hands up as if to show he means us no harm. "Easy."

Faen. Of course, he means no harm. He's Fae, no more capable of harming a Valkyrie than I am. And this girl may have been born three hundred years too late, but she's one of the strongest Valkyrie I've ever met. The blood of her foremothers runs strong in her veins.

"*Beklager*," I murmur my apology to Malachi, forcing the possessive, protectiveness down into a little box. I can examine it later, marvel at it when she isn't in danger. It takes everything I have to force it down, but somehow, I manage it. "I wasn't thinking."

"No harm, no foul. But we need to go," he says. "Half the neighborhood heard him screaming."

Ja, they did. Right before she burned him to ash with nothing more than the Light of her soul.

I glance back down at her, still reeling at the power of her Light. My cock still hard at the sight of her. Gods.

She's extraordinary. She's young and innocent, her soul untouched by shadow.

"We need to get the fuck out of here," Reaper says from behind us. "Half the people inside heard whatever just happened out here."

"Forsaken," Damrion growls.

"*Skíta*. Here?"

"*Ja*. Trying to kidnap the Valkyrie."

I rise to my feet with her in my arms, turning to face my brothers. All four turn curious gazes on her. I fight the urge to snarl at them, instead tucking her carefully against my chest. No one says anything for a long moment. They just stare at her, at us, as if shaken by the sight of her in my arms.

"Don't touch her." I don't know if I can control myself if anyone tries.

They nod as one, not questioning the command.

Sirens ripping through the night shake them from whatever burdens their minds. I can guess the direction of their thoughts anyway.

She looks nothing like the Valkyrie who dedicated their lives to ferrying souls across the Veil, taking pride of place in Valhalla with the warriors they brought home to defend the realms. And yet she may be the strongest who ever lived.

If the other four are even half as strong, the prophecy didn't just spin out the women meant to reopen the portal and restore balance. It spun out the five strongest Valkyrie ever recorded to stand against the Dark. It spun out the brightest Lights the realms have ever known.

If they fail, the nine realms fall to darkness. There is no battle after. No next coming. No more chances. This is it.

And somehow, her soul is bound to mine. There's a reason Odin decreed that the Valkyrie and Fae would never be soul-bound. I'm no more capable of letting her put herself in danger to fulfill her sacred duty than I am of wielding my *lyststål* to end her life.

It's the Fae way. It's always been the Fae way, as much a part of who we are as the power we wield or the Light we shine into the realms. It is who we are at our core. And my brothers know it just as much as I.

To protect her, I'll let the realms burn.

"Adriel, Malachi, take Dax and the Valkyrie in the SUV," Damrion says, stepping forward. "Reaper and I will draw attention away until you're safely out of the city with her."

Reaper grins, always down to be a distraction for the cops. I think he gets off on taunting the human authorities. He's been doing it for centuries.

I stride with my Valkyrie toward the Forsaken's SUV, climbing through the door he tried to push her through just a few short minutes ago. She doesn't stir or make a sound. Malachi jogs around to the passenger side before climbing in, leaving Adriel to drive.

He slams the door behind him, meeting my gaze in the rearview mirror. He doesn't say anything. For several long moments, no one speaks.

And then Malachi mutters a curse. "Since neither of you want to say it, I will. The Forsaken walk the earth again."

"*Ja*. And a Valkyrie soul-bound a Fae," Adriel adds softly.

My gaze falls to the woman sleeping in my arms, my heart thudding against my breastbone hard enough that I feel it for the first time in millennia.

"*Ja*," I whisper. "A Valkyrie soul-bound a Fae."

Chapter Two

Rissa

"V ALKYRIE. *ELSKAN-LJÓS*."

Something warm drifts down the side of my face, pulling me toward the surface. Except I'm more comfortable than I've ever been in my life, and I don't want to rejoin the land of the living. Not yet. I was having good dreams.

Those don't come often.

Usually, I dream of terrible things that leave me gasping for breath and shivering in the dark. Wars and death and a plague of evil falling over the land. I've had the same dreams since I was a little girl. They used to terrify me. Now, I just wish they'd stop.

"Wake up, *elskan-ljós*."

I groan, burying my face in my pillow. A rich, masculine scent tickles my nose. It's all over my pillow, as if someone other than me has been sleeping in my bed. Except there hasn't been anyone. There never has been.

At twenty-one, I've never even been kissed. Tragic, I know. But when you grow up the way I did, there are more important things than dating, boys, and losing the V-Card. You know, things like stability, shelter, and survival.

"Elskan-ljós."

Strands of hair shift away from my face as a large, rough hand drifts gently down my cheek.

My eyes pop open on a gasp, my heart slamming against my ribcage as reality rips the last, lingering vestiges of sleep away. I sit upright in the bed, expecting to find myself alone and dreaming in my tiny little room in my tiny apartment in Seattle.

I'm not. There's nothing familiar in the room around me. I've never seen the hand-hewn cedar dresser, nor the thick fur pelts stretched across the gleaming wooden floor. The giant bed beneath me isn't mine. And the massive, fiercely beautiful man standing over me, his hand still raised as if to touch me again, definitely didn't pop out of my miniscule closet.

I scurry away from him across the bed, putting as much distance between us as I can. "Don't touch me," I gasp, brandishing a pillow like a weapon.

Great. I'm sure he's very intimidated by my choice of weaponry. If I ask nicely, maybe he'll even lay still so I can smother him to death with it.

"Easy, Valkyrie. I won't harm you." His voice is a wet dream, deep and deliciously dark. It sinks deep, stroking places it has no business touching. A thread of command compels me to listen and trust him. To believe he means what he says.

But I trust no one. Not anymore. That ship sank in the Mariana Trench a decade ago, right about the time I learned that the worst pain comes most often from those closest to you.

"Don't come any closer."

His brows furrow over arresting green eyes, his expression turning uncertain. "You don't remember me."

Remember him? I've never even seen him before no—

A flicker of memory floats up from the dark recesses of my mind, halting the denial in its tracks. The memory is incomplete, entire sections of it missing. But enough floats free for me to be certain of two things.

One, I have seen this man before. And two, he's already lied to me.

"You kidnapped me from the bar."

"Kidnapped?" His lips purse as if the word tastes sour upon them. "Is that what you believe, Valkyrie?"

Do I?

I press my fingers to my forehead, trying to think. Why can't I think? Why can't I remember?

"We met at the bar." I look to him for confirmation, though I don't really need it. I know I was at the bar. That, I remember clearly. Genevieve and Jessa dragged me out to celebrate my birthday. Only, like usual, my coworkers ran off to dance with two guys from the office across from ours, and I was left to my own devices.

A stranger kept me company at the bar while I finished my drink. When he found out it was my birthday, he insisted on buying me another drink. Was it this man? I scrutinize him, trying to remember. He doesn't strike me as the kind of person you forget. There's something about him that fascinates me.

It's not his overly long black hair or green eyes. It's not his striking, ruggedly beautiful features. It's not even the fact that, thanks to a trick of the light, he seems to glow faintly. It's a sense of rightness and belonging, as if he's nestled into some deep-down place inside of me and taken up residence.

I don't know how else to explain it. But yesterday, I knew with absolute certainty that I was alone in this world. I was the keeper of my owl soul, the forger of my own destiny. But with this man close, I'm faced with the unshakable realization that I was dead wrong yesterday.

It's almost as if I *feel* him burrowing deep into some corner of my soul that he's carved out just for himself. The thought is pure madness, yet with his eyes on me, I feel it anyway. It's disconcerting as hell.

There's no such thing as soulmates. There's no such thing as destiny. And even if there were, mine certainly isn't at the hands of a handsome man who kidnapped me from a bar.

But I add another certainty to my list. This *isn't* the man who bought me a drink last night. I remember nothing about that man. It's as if a shadow sat beside me, one indistinguishable from every other shadow. He has no shape, no face, no features. Nothing.

I give up trying to remember him and move on.

"I fainted?"

"*Nei*, Valkyrie. You did not." My handsome captor's lips twist, his stance rigid. He's intimidating, standing with his feet planted and his arms crossed over his massive chest. His simple blue t-shirt stretches across the broad wall of his chest, clinging to every muscle beneath. "You were drugged."

"You *drugged* me?" I hiss, jumping to my feet as indignation courses through me. "Oh, I can't wait to smother you with this freaking pillow!"

His gaze drops to the pillow in my hands, a lazy smile turning up the right side of his mouth. "I much prefer when you're sleeping on the pillow, *elskan-ljós*."

"Then you shouldn't have drugged and kidnapped me," I say, my voice saccharine. "Because I don't care what you prefer. I *don't* plan to be a good little prisoner."

Maybe I shouldn't antagonize a man who has already proven he's willing to drug and kidnap me, but I can't help myself. Being silent isn't in my nature. I learned a long time ago to stand up for myself. I've faced bullies before. I've survived the unthinkable. I'll survive this man, too. He may be three times my size, but I'll fight him every step of the way before I just roll over and give up.

"I didn't drug you. Nor are you a prisoner here."

"Really? Then you'll let me leave right now?"

His jaw clenches tight, giving me my answer before he ever speaks a word.

"I didn't think so," I say flatly.

"The man you set on fire in the alley drugged you, *elskan-ljós*. There are more like him out there."

"The man I...?" I stare at him in horror. "I didn't set anyone on fire!"

Good grief. Maybe he isn't a crazy axe-wielding murderer. He's mentally ill. It doesn't excuse him drugging and kidnapping me, of course. But it gives me hope that maybe he doesn't want to hurt me. Maybe he thinks he's helping me.

"*Ja*, you did. Last night."

"No, I..." Another flicker of memory resurfaces, even more incomplete than the last. A pale face surrounded by dark shadow. A cold hand around my throat. This man's face surrounded by a radiant light as the pale man screams a shrill, pain-filled sound and goes up in flames.

The memories are brutal, but the sudden, unshakable knowledge that he isn't lying is even worse. I killed that man. Worse, I wanted him dead. In that moment, with his hand around my throat, I wanted him howling in agony.

My God. He's not lying.

I fling the pillow, diving for the small trashcan beside the bed as my stomach turns. I land on my knees beside it, pulling it into my arms just in time to vomit up everything in my stomach.

My eyes water as the leftover alcohol and nachos reemerges, pouring from my lips into the trashcan.

"*Faen*," my handsome captor says. "Forgive me, Valkyrie. I shouldn't have told you that way." He says it as if there's some easier way to inform someone that they murdered someone.

God. I murdered a man.

If hell is real, I guess I will see my father there someday, after all.

I lower the trashcan, wiping my hand across the back of my mouth.

"Here." My captor appears at my side, taking the trashcan and handing me a bottle of water. "Drink this. You'll feel better."

That's unlikely. But I obediently twist off the cap and take a drink to rinse my mouth, too numb to argue. "Thank you." I hand it back to him.

He sets it on the nightstand built into the bedframe before holding his hand out as if to help me up.

I eye it for a long moment, half afraid of what he might do if I allow him to touch me...and half afraid of what *I* might do. I can't cry right now. I won't.

I carefully place my hand in his, jolting when a current of electricity rushes up my arm, plunging deep into my veins. His little corner in my soul yawns wider. I feel him as he pulls me to my feet, more strongly than I've ever felt anything.

I don't know what he's thinking. I can't read his mind. But it's as if I know what's in his heart. A pervasive, piercing ache. A sense of awe. Need so intense it makes my legs quiver. Dear God, it's so strong it's nearly overwhelming.

Desire surges through me in response, hot and fast, igniting me from the inside out. My core temperature rises, my gaze flying to his.

"Valkyrie," he groans, his deep voice guttural. The green of his eyes seems to swirl with light, growing bright. He pulls me up against his chest, his hard body hot against mine. "Ah, Gods."

I jerk out of his hold, quickly putting distance between us. My God...who *is* this man?

Nei, lyseste lys. He was no man.

Oh. Are you?

The snippet of conversation floats back to me like a bubble popping. What was his response? I search my mind for the answer, but it doesn't come.

What did he mean, the man I killed was no man?

I'm almost afraid to ask.

"Rissa," I whisper.

"Hmm?"

"You keep calling me Valkyrie. My name is Rissa."

"Rissa," he whispers as if testing it out.

I shiver, wrapping my arms around myself and trying like hell not to soften toward this man. Everything in me screams to unbend, to trust. I can't.

"I'm Adaxiel. Everyone calls me Dax."

Adaxiel. Dax. The name fits him.

"If I ask where we are, will you tell me?" I turn back to face him. He's right where I left him, his feet rooted to the spot. "Or am I not allowed to know that?"

"We're in Eitr, Rissa."

"Eitr?" The name tickles the back of my mind. "Why do I know that name?"

"It's a little town in the Cascades a few hours outside of Seattle."

"No." I shake my head, a frown overtaking my face as I concentrate. There are countless dozens of tiny towns in the Cascades, places no one has never and will never hear about. They certainly aren't on any map. People don't move into the deepest, darkest recesses of the mountains out here because they want to be found. Which doesn't give me much hope that this man actually means it when he says I'm not a prisoner here. He doesn't have to tie me up to keep me here. A remote town with an odd name in the Cascades in winter is the next closest thing to a dungeon for someone unfamiliar with the terrain. "That's not it."

He sighs, a long-suffering sigh.

I flick my gaze up at him, my eyes narrowed. "You kidnapped me. If you don't like my questions, that sucks for you."

"It's not your questions, Valkyrie," he says quietly. "It's your stubborn refusal to accept an answer as it's given. You've been awake for all of five minutes. You should rest a while. Then we'll talk."

"Or we talk now, and then I'll decide if I'm capable of resting in this place," I say instead, refusing to back down. Call me crazy, but I don't particularly feel like kicking back in bed and taking it easy right now.

He scowls at me.

I scowl back.

"Gods, you're just like them," he mutters with a sharp shake of his head and an exasperated laugh before he softens. "You take no prisoners, Rissa."

"It's hard to take prisoners when you are one," I say sweetly.

"You aren't a prisoner."

"Says you. But no one drove you to the middle of nowhere while you were unconscious, now did they?"

He growls at me.

"What's Eitr, and why don't you want to tell me?"

"It's a poison made in one of the nine realms."

"Nine realms?" I blink, trying to put the pieces together. "You mean Norse mythology." Of course. That's why it sounds familiar. When I was a little girl, my mother used to fill my head with stories of the Northern people and their Gods. She had this book we read from. Every night was a different adventure.

Honestly, it's no wonder I've had nightmares my whole life. Most of those stories were full of death and dying and wars, things far beyond my understanding at the time. I don't remember much about them now, but I remember the nine realms.

There was Álfheim, Jötunheim, Helheim, Asgard, Midgard, Muspelheim, Svartálfaheim, Niflheim, and Vanaheim, each sitting at different levels on Yggdrasil, the world tree. Most were home to different races of beings. Some of those beings were considered good, and others were anything but, like the giants and the dark elves.

"Eitr!" I snap my fingers as I realize why the name is so familiar. He's right. It was poison. "It was the poison that dripped from the ice in Niflheim and created Ymir, the first being."

"*Ja.*" Dax's eyes glow with pride, making my heart flutter. "The poison that brought life to the world. You know the Norse people, Rissa?"

"A little." I shrug. "My mom used to read bedtime stories to me. Those were always her favorite."

"She must have been Blooded too."

"Blooded?"

"You don't know who you are, do you?"

"Clarissa Michaelson." I grimace, bending to scoop the pillow from the floor where I dropped it. "If you call me Clarissa, though, we're going to have problems you don't want, Adaxiel."

A hint of a smile ghosts across his face. "That's not what I meant, Valkyrie. I meant your history. You don't know it."

My grip tightens around the pillow, my stomach churning. I know my history. I lived every miserable moment of it. But I'm not sharing those wounds with this man. Beautiful as he may be, he's still a—possibly mentally ill—stranger who kidnapped me. That doesn't make him my friend.

"I'm not telling you my life story, Dax," I say flatly. "If that's your kink, you've got the wrong girl. Find someone else."

"My kink?"

"The dirty thing that gets your dic—"

"I know what a kink is, Valkyrie," he growls, eyes narrowing on me. "Bondage. Domination. Watching people fuck in public. Pain." His gaze rakes down my body, his green eyes glowing with an unholy light I like far, far too much. "Believe me, *bittesmå ljós*. You'll be the first to know when I discover what I like."

My stomach quivers. With nerves. With excitement. With an unholy desire to know exactly what his kink is. I hate how much it doesn't quiver with fear. Not once have I truly feared this man. Either I'm a bigger idiot than I thought, or I have a death wish. Because he's death incarnate. I see it in his eyes, glowing like unholy fire. He could rip me apart with his bare hands if he wanted to do it. I think he's probably done exactly that too many times to remember...killed with his bare hands.

He's lethal, the same way lions at rest are lethal. They may let you look. They may even let you get close enough to think you can touch. But as soon as you think you're safe, they strike you down. This man is dangerous. And I don't fear him nearly enough.

God help me. I'm not sure I fear him at all.

Chapter Three

Dax

Rissa is nothing like I expected. Asleep, she looked like one of the beings human's call angels, so peaceful and still. Awake, she's a fierce little warrior, full of suspicion and hellfire. She doesn't give an inch and keeps her guard firmly in place.

She's phenomenal...fascinating in a way no human ever has been to me. Already, I ache for her in ways I can't put into words. I want her in my arms, in my bed, consumed by me. I ache to feel her all over me, coming apart for me. I want every piece of her, body and soul. And I want to give her every piece of me. The desire is intense—growing hotter the longer I stand here.

Does she know it's her Valkyrie blood that gives her such fierce courage? Most in her shoes would be in tears by now. Not Rissa. Sooner or later, she'll crack. They always do. But for now, she's still standing, demanding answers I'm not entirely convinced she's ready to hear.

I understand her need to have those answers, however. I've always preferred to know my odds, too. I'm not an idealist. I don't believe in false hope. The cold, hard truth is better than a sweet lie any day of the week. At least then, I die on my feet, having made my own choices.

I think those are just as important to Rissa. Choices. Making them for herself. I don't understand why yet, but I will. I'll know her better than I know myself. Every part of her will belong to me...and every part of me will be hers. Entire sections of my soul are already falling to her Light.

"I wasn't talking about your personal history, Rissa," I say, leaning against the wall as she clutches my pillow as if it's a shield. "I meant your family history."

She flinches at the mention of her family, just like she did when she mentioned her mom. I file that away for later.

"I have no family."

"Your mom is dead?"

She jerks her head in a nod.

"Your father?"

"I have no father."

Faen. There's a thread of venom in her voice more poisonous than the blood flowing through the veins of the Forsaken. Her father hurt her deeply. If he still walks this earth, he'll pay in blood for whatever he did to her. I'll ensure it. Not because she called my soul but because some horrors are unforgivable. I think whatever happened to her may be one of those unforgivable horrors.

But we're not talking about her father right now. I don't think she'd tell me if I asked. She doesn't trust me yet. Because of him? Perhaps.

"Do you know who the Valkyrie are?"

"Mythical beings who carry the souls of fallen warriors to Valhalla."

"Close," I sigh, pinching the bridge of my nose. Of course she only knows the miniscule little scrap that humanity didn't lose to time. That's not her fault, but it is inconvenient. This would be far easier if she knew even a tenth of the story. "The Valkyrie were a group of powerful beings who carried the souls of the dead across the Veil and maintained the cosmic balance. Fallen warriors who died in battle were given a place of honor in Valhalla." I pause. "If they were soul-bound to a Valkyrie."

"Soul-bound? What does that mean?"

"It means not every warrior who died in battle made it to Valhalla. Unless a Valkyrie called their souls, they never passed through the portal."

"And they had to be bound to a Valkyrie to be called?" she confirms.

"*Ja*. It's the only way they heard the call."

"Why?"

"It was Odin's way of ensuring those who passed through the portal could never bring harm to the Valkyrie." Their numbers were always too few to risk them needlessly. And with every battle, their numbers grew fewer still. They were the greatest Light the realms had against the Dark. And we never had nearly enough of it. Every flame that flickered out allowed Darkness to encroach, leaving thousands of souls at risk.

The Forsaken knew this. They counted on it. The Valkyrie were always their targets. Those souls were always their goal. And the Æsir were too busy fighting amongst themselves to protect the Valkyrie the way they needed to be protected.

Odin did what he could. So did the Fae. *Álfheimr* fell so Valhalla would stand. Because we knew it was far more important than the land that birthed us. But in the end, not even that was enough to keep the flame burning.

"So what happened if their souls weren't called?" Rissa asks.

"The Valkyrie ferried them to Helheim."

She scowls at me. "Well, that's rude."

I blink at her, not understanding.

"They die in battle, don't get to go to Valhalla, and have to go to hell? Rude."

A smile twists at my lips. "Helheim isn't hell, Rissa."

"Uh, it says hell right there in the name, Dax."

"*Ja*, but Helheim existed long before any concept of hell that you know, *elskan-ljós*. Helheim is simply the afterlife. For most, it's neither a place of torment nor a haven. It's merely a place where life continues on in some form. Only those mired in Darkness find Helheim unwelcoming."

"Fine, so they go to Not-Hell," she grumbles, finally loosening her grip on the pillow. It's misshapen now, all the feathers having escaped to the ends. She doesn't notice. "And the Valkyrie soul-bound the warriors they found worthy because Odin decided that was the way. What does this have to do with the price of tea in China?"

"It has nothing to do with the price of tea in China."

The tiniest of smiles dances across her lips. "It's a saying, Dax. It means I think you're telling me pointless, irrelevant things."

"Ah, I see." I push away from the wall, taking a tentative step in her direction. She doesn't immediately back away from me. A good sign. I need to be close to her. "Two thousand years ago, most of the Valkyrie were killed in the Final Battle."

"You mean Ragnarök?"

I nod. "With so few left to ferry souls across, the Forsaken started snatching them. Thousands upon thousands of souls, destroyed by an evil you can't even begin to comprehend."

"Wait. Who are the Forsaken, and why do they want souls?"

"They're an ancient evil. One that predates anything you know." I hesitate. "I suppose they're the original concept of evil. Religion never gets it right considering not even the Gods would reveal where they came from, but religion tries to explain their existence the best it can."

"And they want souls because that's just their thing?"

"*Nei*. They feed off them."

"Gross." She scrunches up her face. "So, ancient soul-eaters."

"It's more complicated than that. Souls are power. They feed off the power for their dark magic. But *ja*, that's the gist of it."

"This was so not in the book my mom read," she mutters.

"It would not have been. The Æsir forbade any mention of the Forsaken on earth."

"Why?"

"Look what people have done with your devil," I murmur. "They exalt him as if evil deeds and the subjugation of the soul are something to aspire to. Do you think it would have gone differently with the Forsaken? The Æsir wouldn't risk starting a cult of willing disciples. Better to pretend the Forsaken didn't exist at all than to risk giving them an army of followers."

Rissa's brow furrows as she considers this. She's silent for a moment before she nods, swallowing hard. "Yeah," she whispers. "I guess you're right."

"The Valkyrie who were left after Ragnarök knew they had to do something to stop the Forsaken, so those who weren't bound to a warrior began to lay with humans."

"Lay with? You mean sleep with, right?"

"*Ja*. Sleep with." I take another step toward her. "They hoped to bolster their numbers by birthing Valkyrie capable of joining their ranks."

"Did it work?"

I shake my head. "Something else happened instead."

"What?"

"They set in motion a prophecy that will save the nine realms forever. Or destroy them for eternity."

She absorbs this quietly, her lips slightly parted.

"Your great-great-great-great grandmother, many times removed, is the daughter of one of those Valkyrie, *elskan-ljós*."

She laughs abruptly. "You almost had me for a minute there, Dax."

"The man you set on fire last night was Forsaken, Rissa," I growl. Valkyrie were always stubborn and willful. They never liked to listen. Apparently, they still don't. "Others will be coming for you. They won't stop until you're too powerful for them to stand against."

"And the Valkyrie sent you to kidnap me for my own protection, right?"

"The Valkyrie are dead!"

She flinches backward, her face paling. Her laughter fades, silenced by my roar. I immediately feel like a *drittsekk,* an asshole, for shouting at her. It's not her fault she doesn't understand. None of this is her fault. But her life is in danger, and I need her to take that seriously. It's the only way she survives. And more than anything—more than Valhalla or the portal or the prophecy—I need her to survive. Our bond demands it. *I* demand it.

That's my priority now. That's what I'll give my life to protect. *Her*. Even if it means watching the realms fall to Darkness. The minute she called my soul, she became mine. I'll do anything, even destroy my own soul to keep her Light shining.

"The Forsaken murdered every remaining Valkyrie three hundred years ago, Rissa," I say, more calmly than I feel. I want to go to her, to offer her comfort. I ache to pull her into my arms and hold her together, but I know she won't let me. My Valkyrie is fierce and independent, and right now, she doesn't trust me at all. "They invaded Valhalla and destroyed everything in their path. We've been stranded here since, waiting for the five prophesized to restore the cosmic balance." I take a final step toward her, this one putting me within reach of her. I place my hand beneath her chin, tipping her face up to mine.

She doesn't flinch from me. She doesn't run screaming. Her gaze flickers across my face, her blue eyes wide and solemn, as if she's trying to work out for herself if I'm being honest or if I've lost my mind.

"We've been waiting for you, Valkyrie."

"No," she whispers, shaking her head. "No."

"*Ja*. Yes."

"I'm not who you think I am. I'm not *what* you think I am."

"You're Valkyrie, *my* Valkyrie." I curl my hands into fists, fighting the urge to pluck her into my arms. Fighting my nature. Gods. I want to kiss her.

"Y-your Valkyrie?" The tip of her tongue darts out, sweeping along her bottom lip.

I fight the urge to groan at the sight of it. Fight the desire to dip my head and taste it for myself. Gods, how I crave her. In ways so profound, they defy description.

"D-Dax, what are you? Are you one of those warriors?"

Neither is the question I expected her to ask.

"*Nei*, Rissa. I'm not."

"But you aren't human, either."

"*Nei*."

"Tell me."

"My brothers and I are Fae, the oath-sworn Guardians of Valhalla."

"B-brothers? How many of you are there?"

"167. The last of the Fae." I pause. "The last flickering flame of Valhalla."

"And you're all stranded here? On earth?"

"*Ja*."

She expels a soft breath, which shakes upon her lips. "And you think I'm one of the Valkyrie you're looking for?"

"I know you are, Rissa."

"How?"

"Because you are."

"How do you know?"

"I feel it." I tap my chest, right over my heart. "Here."

Her gaze follows my hand. "A-are you s-saying...?"

Ja, little Valkyrie. That's exactly what I'm saying. You called my soul.

I lean forward, brushing my lips across her forehead instead of answering her question. She isn't ready. Not now. Not yet. If I tell her that truth, it'll shatter whatever trust she's decided to give me. I don't have to know her to know that. I see it in her eyes. Accepting the truth about Valkyrie and Forsaken and the fate of the world is one thing. But accepting that her soul is tied to mine? That thought terrifies the hell out of this little warrior.

War, she's willing to accept. But love? She'd rather run screaming into the night.

When I find out who hurt her so badly she built a fortress around her heart, Gods have mercy on their soul. I certainly won't have any.

"Rest, Valkyrie. We'll talk again when you've had time to process."

I step away from her, striding toward the door.

"Dax."

"The fire last night. Um, the one that killed that...that Forsaken," she whispers behind me. "I really started it, didn't I?"

"*Ja.*"

"I killed him."

"*Nei*, Rissa. You can't kill what's already dead. You protected yourself. That's all."

She sighs, a forlorn, devastating sound that shatters my heart. I turn to cross back to her, unable to leave when everything in me demands I comfort her. But I'm not even half a step before she throws up a hand, halting me.

"Please, just go," she whispers.

It kills me to give her what she demands, but she holds my bond. I'm no more capable of defying her order than I am of harming a single hair on her head. I protect her above all things, even when it means protecting her from me. Our bond frightens her. I frighten her. Right now, I'm the enemy. I fucking hate it, but to her, it's true.

"I'll be downstairs if you need me."

She crawls onto the bed, not speaking.

My last glimpse of her is of tears shimmering in her lashes, my pillow gripped to her chest as if she's trying to draw it into herself. And for the first time in three hundred years, I feel...sorrow.

Chapter Four

Dax

"You're still alive." Malachi tosses one booted foot up on the coffee table, clasping his fingers together behind his head as he grins at me. "I knew you'd handle the bond well."

"You're full of shit is what you are," Reaper mutters, kicking his foot off the table. It lands on the wooden floor with a thud, jolting Malachi forward in his chair. "You're betting against him."

Malachi's grin grows, his expression unrepentant as he immediately stretches his legs out, unbothered by Reaper. "Yes, well, I'm trying to off-load my share of our fortune before we make a triumphant return to Valhalla."

Despite living simply, we've amassed a small human fortune over the last three centuries. It's not hard to do when you've got nothing but time. We use it only when we must, to ensure the safety of the Fae and the Blooded who find their way to us, or to aid in our mission. Riches have never mattered much to the Fae. When you live forever, they lose their luster.

Several of the Fae, like Malachi, make a game of winning—and losing—vast sums of money. They bet on everything. Including, apparently, whether I can win the heart of my Valkyrie or if I'll fuck it up.

I'm not a patient Fae and I never have been. My brothers know this. And Rissa hasn't left my room in two days. She barely lets me through the door. I do not like living under the same roof with doors closed between us. But I'm trying to give her time to get used to me. She's been through a lot.

That doesn't make me any more of a patient Fae. I'm ready to tear the house down around us to get through those doors to her. It's fucking killing me that she won't let me in. That she's afraid. I feel her pain, her fear, her grief. I feel it all. And there's nothing I can do about any of it. My Valkyrie is drowning in her own mind, and I'm helpless.

Reaper's deep, disbelieving laugh booms across the living room. "How you've survived this long is a mystery, Malachi."

I tune them out, looking at Adriel, who's seated at the dining room table for the first time in days, slowly shuffling through a deck of cards. "Did you get rid of the SUV?"

"Drove it all over the state and then pushed it over a cliff two hours east of here. If they have a tracker on it, it won't lead them here," he answers without looking up.

"Do we have warriors guarding the gates?"

Unlike most towns nestled this deep in the Cascades, ours is a fortress carefully constructed for defense. Two entire blocks are designed to look exactly like every other tiny human town in this part of the world. Those, we allow the world to see. But the rest is carefully hidden behind walls no one is allowed behind unless we decide to let them. Most never even realize that they're even here.

They take what they're shown at face value and don't look deeper.

Those who do see more are usually those who were compelled to come by some force they don't yet understand. The Blooded, we allow through the gates. The rest, we redirect away. They stumble on their way with nothing more than vague memories of a tiny town of secrets.

We don't guard Eitr so closely without reason. Every last Fae will fall before we willingly allow the Forsaken to get their hands on the Blooded who call this place home. They may not be the Valkyrie meant to fulfill the prophecy, but they're Valkyrie enough. We keep our oath, even now. Especially with Abigail here. She's the most powerful Blooded we've ever met. If the Forsaken were to get their hands on her... Well, Gods help us all if she were to fall into their hands.

"And the forest and the valley below and every road that leads anywhere close to here." Adriel stops shuffling, turning that one steely eye on me. "This isn't our first day in the Hall, Dax," he says, referring to the Hall of Warriors. It was a place of honor, and a training ground, the one place in the realms where every man—Fae or human—stood as an equal, ready to defend the Valkyrie.

With Valhalla gone, we've built our own training grounds in the heart of Eitr. It's a cold substitute for the Hall, but we've known three hundred years of peace. Three hundred years for our minds to grow dull and our skills to stagnate. We needed the practice to keep us sharp. The prophecy demands it.

"Never said it was. Where's Damrion?"

"Where else?" Adriel says, disapproval heavy in his tone.

With Abigail, then.

I sigh, biting back another reminder that the girl has no one else. It'll fall on deaf ears if I voice it. Besides, it's not Abigail that Adriel has an issue with. He likes the girl better than he likes most anyone else. He simply can't stand the fact that she idolizes Damrion.

Someday, the two of them will deal with their shit. But today isn't that day. I doubt it'll be tomorrow, either.

I glance toward the stairs, hesitant to leave Rissa here when I promised that I'd be downstairs. But cell service is nonexistent out here. Most of us don't even bother carrying phones because the damn things rarely work. It could be three days before a text goes through—if it goes through at all.

"Go," Adriel says. "I'll guard her."

I hesitate for a moment, not because I don't trust him. He may be a crabby bastard most of the time, but his loyalty is to Valhalla and the Valkyrie. I've never doubted that and never will. Adriel would lay down his life without hesitation to protect Rissa. Rather, I hesitate simply because I don't want to leave.

Already, I feel too far away from her. Already, the bond whispers, compelling me back to her side. Does she feel it, too? Does her skin crawl now that I'm not at her side? Does she recognize it for what it is?

Nei. How could she? To her, soul-binding and ancient Fae warriors and Valhalla are simply stories, fairytales her mother filled her head with when she was a girl. They aren't real life. They aren't *her* life.

Already, I hate what we must ask her to do, the painful truths I've forced her to face over the last few days. She's young, innocent, her past littered with pain. But the Norns never cared about that. They weave as they see fit, never considering the cost to those called.

They never ask if we want to carry the burden they choose us to carry. They simply ensure we're strong enough to heft it. And forging the strength needed to carry those burdens is rarely anything short of painful. But no one ever said the Norns were kind and benevolent. They only promised that they would weave.

Gods know, they haven't been kind to the Fae.

"Guard her close," I growl, stomping toward the door.

"I'll go with you." Reaper rises to his feet, following behind me.

A blast of ice-cold air hits me in the face, bringing bits of ice and flakes of snow with it. I wave them out of my face with a flick of my wrist and step out. No matter how long we're here, the bitter cold is always a shock. It irritates the hell out of me.

"*Eselballer*," Reaper mutters. "It gets colder every day."

"*Ja*. It's winter."

"Smart ass."

I jog down the steps, cutting a path across the frozen grass to the small cabin in front of ours. Our workshops and meeting places and healing rooms and markets line the three blocks that make up the town square. Most of the warriors live in barracks like ours that circle the square in ever-widening rings. The Blooded live in smaller cabins in a tighter ring at the heart, where they're safest. Everything was designed with defense in mind, unlike human cities that sprawl this way and that, leaving the most vulnerable unprotected and at risk.

But warfare in this realm is unlike any other. With their bombs and guns and planes, humans have found an entirely new way to fight war. It's more barbaric in many ways, infinitely more violent, and yet there are rules and niceties to it that don't exist in any other realm. We've studied it closely in the last three hundred years. We never involved ourselves, even when we wished we could.

Humans are complicated creatures, far more complex than anyone thought. It's not hard to see why they've survived when the other realms faded one by one and died. Destroyed by pride and their own foolish belief that they alone could stand against the dark.

Humans, while often arrogant, understand that they aren't invincible. They accept that death comes for everyone eventually. They're far more willing to work as a unit to change the flow of time instead of seeking to have their names written in the stars. That willingness to work together, even when it means working with an enemy, for the greater good, is something no other realm has ever been able to master. Not even the Fae.

"You know destroying the car won't hold them off for long," Reaper says as we near Abigail and Letty's door. "Sooner or later, they're going to find her."

"I know."

"She has to be ready."

"I know," I growl.

"The best thing you can do to protect her is to train her."

"I know that too." I turn to glare at him. "But I can't train her if I can't even convince her that I didn't drug and kidnap her, now can I?"

"*Skita*." Reaper's eyes widen. "She still doesn't remember what happened?"

I hesitate, not sure how to answer that. "Bits and pieces. Enough to make her leery of me." I blow out a breath. "Whatever he gave her wiped big chunks of the night from her memory."

"GHB," Reaper says with a nod. "She's probably familiar enough with it to suspect you doused her drink with it."

I glower at the thought, something dark and deadly twisting through me. If someone doused her with it before, they'll live just long enough to regret it when I find them. No one touches the Valkyrie. No one.

Especially not the fiery little Valkyrie refusing to leave my room.

She's mine.

Abigail and Letty's front door pops open as Reaper and I near the porch. Snow stands two inches deep on the arms of Letty's favorite rocking chair. Icicles hang like stalactites from the eaves and gutters.

The powerful eighteen-year-old Seer bounces out, bundled up in a fluffy coat and gloves, with Damrion hot on her heels. Strands of her wild red hair frame her round face.

"Dax!" She flashes a bright smile at me, her blue eyes fathomless. "Damrion said I could meet the Valkyrie today."

"I did not say that," Damrion rumbles. "I said maybe you could meet her later."

"Same difference." Abigail beams, knowing she'll get her way. Damrion can never tell her no. Neither can Adriel. "Is she as beautiful as she was in my vision, Dax?"

"*Ja*," I say quietly. "Like the sun."

"You love her already."

I eye her, surprised.

She places her hand on my arm. "It's okay. She's going to love you too. Just like Gerðr loved Freyr."

Damrion and Reaper share a look.

"Abigail, *ást-meer*," I say gently. "Did you know that Rissa was going to call my soul?"

"Her name is Rissa?"

"*Ja*, it is."

"Answer him, Abigail," Damrion orders.

"Yes." She glances between the three of us, her expression worried. "But I couldn't see when it happened. I didn't want to say anything in case it didn't happen right away." Her teeth sink into her bottom lip. "Are you mad?"

"*Nei, ást-meer*." I share a look with Reaper, shocked. Never in recorded memory has anyone been able to Foretell a bond, not even the Valkyrie. "But it's important that you tell us everything you see. Even the things you believe are unimportant."

Her teeth sink deeper into her bottom lip. Last year, Adriel caught her outside the gates alone. He wasn't happy. By the time they made it back inside the gates, she was in tears, and he wasn't speaking. She retaliated by filling his bed with frogs, the one thing in this realm the scarred warrior hates. When he discovered them, Abigail wore the same look she's wearing right now. *Guilt.*

"You know something," Reaper says, reading the same thing I do on her face.

"We have to go see Rissa."

"Abigail."

"She's going to try to sneak out the window!" Abigail cries. "I thought if I went to see her, I could convince her not to do it. But if we keep standing here, it'll be too late."

"*Faen*," I growl, spinning on my heel to run back to the house. She's going to break her fool neck. *Nei*. I'm going to spank her perfect ass before she has a chance to do that.

What is she thinking?

Do I even need to ask?

She's fleeing for her life. Literally.

I burst through the front door, hitting it so hard it slams into the wall before flying back at me. I catch it with my shoulder, grunting.

Malachi and Adriel both turn, matching expressions on their faces. I don't stop to explain. Someone else can do that.

I take the stairs two at a time, my steps heavy on the gleaming red cedar. The bedroom door slams against the wall with force.

Rissa jumps a foot into the air, wheeling to face me with one hand over her heart. "Jesus, Dax. I thought you were the freaking police."

"What are you doing?"

"Uh, I was going pee. Is that a problem?"

I stride past her to the window, examining the lock. It hasn't been touched. But Abigail is never wrong. If she saw

Rissa sneaking out the window, it's because my stubborn, infuriating little Valkyrie intends to go out the window.

Well, we're solving that vision here and now.

"Come here."

"Why?"

"Because I want you over here."

"I'm good here, but thanks."

"Now, Valkyrie."

She glowers at me, stubbornly planting her feet.

I take a warning step in her direction.

She quickly decides now isn't the time to test me and scurries across the room to me, stopping just out of my reach. "I'm here. Happy now?"

"Try to climb out of the window."

She blanches. "Are you insane?"

"*Nei*. We both know you were thinking about it."

"Thinking about something and doing it are two different things, Dax. They're called intrusive thoughts. You know, the crazy things we think but don't act on *because they're crazy*?"

"Try, Rissa."

"If you want someone to go out the window so badly, I can push you out," she suggests, batting her lashes at me. "I bet it won't even hurt when you land on your stupid, hot face."

I refuse to back down, though she makes it hard. She's a bright flame. And just like a flame, she burns hot. Her temper is as fierce as any Valkyrie's. But when she loses hers, I want to kiss the fire from her mouth to see how it burns.

"Fine," she says, elbowing me in the stomach as she slips past me to the window. She makes a production of throwing it open, making sure I know she's annoyed with me.

I watch her carefully as she attempts to shimmy her way up onto the sill, only to slip back down again. After the third try, she gives up, spinning to face me.

"If you want me up ther—"

I'm on top of her in a split second, backing her up against the wall. My lips come down on hers, my kiss hard and hungry. Her lips part on a surprised gasp, allowing me entry. I take the unwitting invitation, stealing her breath as she melts into me. She whimpers, throwing her arms around me as she returns my kiss, just as eager, just as hungry.

Heat flows between us, quickly morphing into an inferno.

Gods. Is this how it's to be between us then? Fire and ice? A constant push and pull until we both ignite, too wild with want to contain it any longer? It's Niflheim and Muspelheim all over again, the runoff of two polar opposites crashing together to raise giants.

Only this time, it's Valkyrie and Fae, Light and her Guardian. And not even the Forsaken themselves will be able to pry her from my arms when she finally accepts the bond she forged between us.

I deepen the kiss, my hands running all over her soft body. She's the sun in my arms, fierce and hot. She's a storm, too, wild and untamed. Her sweet sounds send desire spiraling toward madness. My cock aches, desperate to know what it feels like to sink into her heat and get lost. That's where I belong. Lost in this Valkyrie, her soul tangled with mine.

Ah, Gods. I want it. Need it.

I break the kiss, breathing hard. "Believe whatever you want to tell yourself about me, *elskan-ljós*. Convince yourself that none of this is happening if that's what you must do to protect yourself. But *do not ever* put yourself in danger," I snarl against her lips. "Or you'll answer to me."

"I thought you said you wouldn't hurt me."

"*Ja*, I did. But who said spanking you would hurt?"

"You are *not* spanking me." Her voice shakes, but not with fear. With desire.

"Then forget whatever plans you've been up here making. You'll break your fool neck trying to escape out of the window, get lost in the forest, or be eaten by any number of wild animals. We're miles from anything resembling civilization, and I didn't bring you out here to die."

A hysterical laugh bubbles up from her throat. "Yes, you did. That's exactly why you brought me here, Dax. To die fulfilling some prophecy you claim I'm supposed to fulfill."

"*Nei*," I murmur, stroking my thumb down her cheek, trying to soothe her. Her skin is so soft. "Every Fae here will fall to Darkness before we allow you to do so."

She meets my gaze, a question swirling in hers. "Why?"

"Because it's who we are. Because it's our duty. Because you called my soul and gave every single one of us what we haven't had in three hundred years. *Hope*."

She stares at me for a long, silent moment, and then sighs. She doesn't panic at my admission that she called my soul. She doesn't deny it, either. She simply ignores that I brought it up at all. "How did you know I was going to try to sneak out?" Horror and suspicion overtake her gaze. "Can you read my mind?"

"*Nei, elskan-ljós*. That isn't one of the Fae gifts." I brush my thumb across her lip, unable to stop touching her now that I've started. Gods help me. I may never stop.

"Oh." Her shoulders droop, relief coloring her tone. "Then how?"

"Come downstairs, and I'll show you." I hold my hand out, leaving the choice up to her. Praying to the Gods that she takes it.

She hesitates for only a moment before gingerly placing her hand into mine and claiming another piece of my soul.

Chapter Five

Rissa

Dax lives in a fairytale mansion. At least that's how it seems to me. The house was obviously built by hand...his unless I miss my guess. And either he's had practice at it, or working with wood comes naturally to him because every hand-hewn wall stands in testament to the skill and craftmanship that went into it. Every massive log was carefully placed, the seams so tightly compacted that it's hard to tell where one log ends and another begins.

Large windows nestle high up, allowing natural light to flood into every corner. It should be cold inside, considering the thick layer of snow and ice coating everything outside. But it's warm and inviting.

I understand why when we make it down the giant staircase. A fireplace takes up half of one wall, flames dancing from thick pieces of wood inside. Half a dozen people stand around it, staring at us.

My steps falter.

"Easy, *elskan-ljós*," Dax murmurs, his hand at the small of my back. He hovers over me like the world's most protective prison guard. Except I've mostly accepted that he didn't kidnap me and I'm not a prisoner here. I think I may even believe what he told me.

That's what terrifies me. I *believe* him...and I don't want to. I want to go back to a week ago when my life made some semblance of sense. It's never been easy. There have always been little things that made me feel like I didn't quite belong. I've always felt things I shouldn't, heard things that weren't there, but those little whispers never led me astray. Until now.

Aside from one tiny girl who can't be older than sixteen or seventeen, everyone else in the room is just as big and intimidating as Dax. Two of the men—Fae?—seem familiar, as if I should be able to place them.

Were they at the bar the other night, too? I don't remember, but I think they were.

One of them grins at me, humor in his blue eyes. He has ebony skin and braids in his long hair. He's beautiful in a brutal sort of way, but he doesn't look dangerous. I think he probably is, though.

The one beside him screams darkness and danger. He's pale with a single black eye. A vicious scar bisects the other, running halfway down his cheek. He watches me intently, as if he's weighing and measuring the worth of my soul. I'm not sure what he decides, but I quickly shift my gaze from him when he cocks his brow as if to call me out for staring at him.

The man standing closest to the stairs is beautiful. Out of everyone in the room aside from Dax, he's the most human, but there's something about him that's simply different. I've seen beautiful men before. They're everywhere in this world. But this one is too perfectly formed. Too bright. His brown skin gleams. His amber eyes aren't shadowed. There is no cold arrogance in the way he holds himself. Out of everyone in the room, he's the one who looks the most human...yet seems the most Fae.

The final man in the room seems almost deceptively normal compared to the others. He's massive like Dax, with olive skin and gold eyes. There's an air of authority about him, and an endless abundance of patience. He smiles at me when I meet his gaze, his expression kind.

I'm positive every one of them is Fae like Dax. Not the girl, though. She's human like me. She's beaming at me, practically quivering where she stands as if it's taking everything she has not to race forward to introduce herself. I like her immediately.

"Rissa, these are my brothers," Dax says, leading me down the final few stairs. My feet hit the bottom and I stop, refusing to move any further. "Damrion." He points at the Fae who smiled at me. "Adriel." The scarred Fae. "Malachi." The Fae with humor in his eyes. "And Kyvon. We call him Reaper." Reaper gives me a salute. "And this is Abigail."

"Hi," I whisper, my stomach fluttering with nerves. How the heck do you introduce yourself to a room full of warriors you're pretty sure have been alive longer than everyone you've ever met, combined?

"Valkyrie," Damrion says, his voice a deep rumble, like a rockslide.

"Sup, Rissa?" Malachi grins at me.

"*Sup?*" Reaper shoots a scornful look at Malachi. "How *have* you lived this long?"

Malachi hefts his finger in the air, making the human girl giggle.

Damrion shoots a quelling look at the two warriors.

"Hi, Rissa." Abigail skips forward to meet me, flinging her arms out. Before I can react, she pulls me into a fierce hug. "I'm really happy you're finally here. I knew Dax would find you."

"Um...hi." I hug her back, taken off guard by her warmth and exuberance. It's unexpected, especially in a place like this. And then her words register, crashing together with Dax's cryptic comment from earlier that he'd show me how he knew I was thinking about sneaking out of the window. I gasp, pulling back to look at Abigail. "You knew about me?"

"I saw you," she says, bobbing her head. Her red braid bounces with the movement, little baby hairs around her face shifting too. "It's what I do. See things."

"She's a psychic?" I ask, looking to Dax for confirmation.

"She isn't like the humans you see on television, Valkyrie," Adriel growls. "She's a powerful Seer. One of the most powerful we've ever known. What she sees always comes to pass. *Always.*"

I flinch at the rebuke in his tone, as if my question somehow offended him, even though I didn't intend it to be offensive.

"I'm like you," Abigail says, her soft tone a stark contrast to his. "One of my ancestors was a Valkyrie. There are others like us here."

"They see the future too?"

"*Nei, elskan-ljós,*" Dax murmurs, placing his hand on the small of my back again. The weight of it burns me, making my stomach tremble. "Not all. Not even most. Some sense when things are going to happen. Some can predict the weather, or wars. Some are skilled with healing. But most possess no gifts at all."

"There are no others here as strong as Abigail." Malachi meets my gaze. "At least, there weren't."

"Awesome," I say with false enthusiasm. So I guess that means I'm as much an oddball here as I have been my whole life. It's an uncomfortable realization. One I should be used to by now, I suppose. But when you've always been the weird one, the one who sensed things no one else did, people always look at you differently. No matter how hard you try to fit in, you always stand out anyway. I guess I get to do that here, too.

I don't relish it. For once in my life, I don't want to be the girl with a dead mom and a murderous father. I don't want to be a freak of nature. I just want...what? I've never known exactly how to answer that question. It's like the answer is on the tip of my tongue, but it eludes me.

Dax shifts beside me, and my gaze flickers in his direction. Even in profile, he's one of the most handsome men I've ever met, so fierce and radiant. Like the sunrise on a battlefield.

An answer bubbles up from deep within my soul. One that terrifies and excites me in equal measure.

Him. I want him.

I want his lips on mine again like they were upstairs.

I shake my head, trying to dislodge the thought, but it refuses to budge. It's in there now, stuck. He's in there now, burrowing deeper the longer I'm here. I didn't tell him, but that's why I wanted to flee. Not because of Valhalla or the Forsaken or any of the not-quite-believable things he told me. But because, out of all of them, he's the thing that scares me the most.

I don't want to fall for him. I don't want to need him.

Love is pain. I learned that lesson early. My father taught it well, over and over, until his kind of love killed my mom, leaving me alone in a world that didn't want me. Opening myself to this man feels like opening a vein. Only, I might just bleed out this time. Because there's something about him that makes me want to open it.

How is that possible when I don't even know him?

Because your soul is bound to his. Might as well accept it, dummy.

I ignore that little voice, ignore the implications. What other choice do I have?

I know what he wants from me. Fate of souls and worlds and the whole dang universe.

If this is adulthood, I'd like to cancel my subscription, please.

"Are you hungry, *elskan-ljós*?"

My stomach growls at the mention of food.

Malachi laughs loudly, making me blush. I guess he heard that, then.

"Come. I'll feed you." Dax leads me across the living room toward the kitchen. Like the rest of the house, it's beautiful. Granite and cedar dazzle me everywhere I look, as if the room sprang up from the mountainside. Even the modern appliances blend into the room, the stove and industrial-sized chrome fridge somehow complementing everything else. It's far more functional than I expected for a home this cut off from civilization.

"If I ask exactly where in the Cascades we are, would you tell me?" I question, perching on a wooden stool at a massive center island.

Abigail, who followed us in, hops up onto a stool beside me while Dax crosses to the fridge, pulling it open to rummage around.

"We're close to the volcano," she says. "When it isn't snowing, you can see the top of the peak. Sometimes, you can even see it venting steam."

"Mt. Rainer?"

"Mt. Baker."

I blink, surprised. We're even deeper in the mountains than I thought...and much further from Seattle than I expected. Mt. Baker is the highest peak in the state, a little over three hours from Seattle. Most of the roadways around Mt. Baker are virtually impassable during the winter months. Even major highways shut down, leaving travel through certain areas a crapshoot.

"This is where the portal sent the Fae when Valhalla fell," Abigail explains. "Damrion says they built the Hall on the exact spot to honor the Fae who died in the collapse."

"About that," I say to Dax, watching as he pulls items out of the fridge, creating a rapidly growing pile in his arms. "What is this portal, and what happened to it?"

"Have you heard of the Bifröst?"

"Yes." It was, supposedly, a rainbow bridge that allowed the Gods to travel between realms.

"The portal was a piece of the Bifröst tying Valhalla to Asgard," Dax says without turning around. "The rest of the Bifröst was destroyed during the Final Battle, leaving the realms cut off from one another, but the portal remained hidden deep within Asgard."

"Until the Forsaken found it," Abigail says, her voice dark.

"*Ja*," Dax agrees. "Three hundred years ago, the Forsaken poured into Valhalla without warning. They massacred thousands. We assumed they came for the Valkyrie. They'd certainly spent long enough hunting them across the realms. But the portal was their goal. They unleashed their magic upon it, cutting Valhalla off from Asgard."

"Dax and the Fae tried to stop them, but when they went through the portal, for the first time ever, it didn't lead them to Asgard. It brought them here. Dozens of Fae were still inside when the portal collapsed." Abigail's blue eyes well with sorrow for the Fae who died within the portal. "They died horribly."

I slip my hand into hers, offering her comfort. Praying this isn't something she saw in one of her visions. She's just a girl. She may live amongst warriors and see things no one else sees, but at the end of the day, she's still just a girl. There are some horrors she shouldn't know.

Dax nudges the door of the fridge closed with his foot, turning to deposit his pile of ingredients on the island in front of us. Lettuce, tomato, cheese, meats, a loaf of fresh bread... There's enough to feed a small army. "Is a sandwich satisfactory, Valkyrie? Adriel will stick his *lyststål* up my ass if I fuck up the kitchen again."

"Dax is a messy cook," Abigail whispers conspiratorially. "*Lyststål?*"

Dax grins, taking a step away from the counter. He doesn't do anything else that I can tell, but I feel power suddenly rush into him from all around, as if the very air in the room suddenly flows to him. As it does, the faint glow around him grows brighter and then brighter still. He makes a lazy motion with his hand, like he's flipping it over to present something with a flourish. A blazing sword suddenly appears, clutched in his giant fist.

I rear back, startled at its sudden appearance.

"Easy, Rissa," he murmurs gently, holding the massive sword of light aloft. "I won't hurt you."

"It's..." I stare in fascination at the gleaming weapon in his hands. I know nothing about swords, but this one seems massive, reaching almost to the ceiling even though he holds it at waist level. The handle curves at the end, fitting his hand as if it were made just for him. It's not the first time I've seen the glowing weapon. "You had this at the bar."

"*Ja.*"

The wickedly sharp weapon is formed entirely from light, yet it's steel, too. I don't understand how that's possible, but there's no denying the reality when it's right in front of me. This is no trick, no sleight of hand. The weapon is as real as the Fae standing in front of me.

"Can I touch it?"

"*Nei.*" He pulls it back as if worried I might try. "The *lyststål* burns everything it touches." He holds his arm out, gently placing the edge of the sword to it. His flesh immediately turns red.

"Dax!" I cry, jumping to my feet.

"Easy, Valkyrie. Easy." He waves his hands, and the weapon vanishes. A rivulet of blood runs down his arm from the angry red wound it left behind. He grabs a paper towel from the roll and dabs at it.

"Are you insane?" I scowl daggers at him.

Abigail giggles beside me.

"I'm well, Rissa." He pulls the paper towel away from the wound. "The *lyststål* will burn Fae flesh as easily as they do anything else, but only we wield them for a reason."

"Because you're insane and enjoy pain?" I snap at him.

He merely grins at me, warmth in his eyes.

"The weapon is part of the Fae who calls it," Abigail explains. "The burns are only temporary on Fae flesh because the weapon is formed of their Light. That's why it's called a *lyststål*, or lightsword. See?" She points at his arm. "It's already healing."

I glance at his arm and then do a double-take. She's right. The wound is healing. Already, the angry red has faded to pink, as if the wound is weeks old instead of mere moments.

He tosses the paper towel into the trash can, washes his hands, and then returns to making sandwiches as if nothing happened. I watch him for several long moments as the wound heals completely, vanishing as if it were never there at all.

A thousand questions battle for dominance, but I don't know which is the most pressing. All of them seem urgent. All of them seem important.

"You were upset," he murmurs after a moment.

"What?"

"You were upset when you thought I was injured." His green eyes flicker to mine, emotion swirling through them. "You worried for me."

"I..." I trail off before the denial forms, unable to voice it. Instead, I shrug like it's not a big deal. "I'm still partially convinced you're a crazy person, and this is all some story you've convinced yourself is real."

He sighs quietly. "It would be easier if it were."

"Yeah, I guess it would." My lips pull down into a frown as I face the dawning realization that I don't want this to be some dream or nightmare or made-up fairytale. I don't want to wake up to find out he was just a figment of my imagination.

Already, he's growing on me. He feels...important...to me. Because of the bond? I'm still not sure I believe that part—or that I want to believe it. But I can't deny that there's something growing between the two of us. It's like I'm staring at the sun with my eyes closed, its brightness beating against my eyelids. I can't see it, but I feel it all the same.

"Dax," Abigail says suddenly. "Something is wrong."

I glance at her to see her swaying on the stool, her face stark white. She's staring right at Dax, but I don't think she's seeing him. It's as if she's looking right through him, seeing something happening worlds away.

Every hair on my body stands on end, a cold chill ripping through me.

"*Faen!*" Dax growls, dropping the loaf of bread as he launches himself over the island. He grabs her by the shoulders, gently lifting her from the stool. "Damrion! *Kom inn hit!*"

He lowers her to the floor, kneeling beside her.

"What can I do?" I ask as her eyes roll back in her head, and she begins to thrash, fighting his hold. "How can I help?"

"Talk to her, *elskan-ljós*," Dax says. "Comfort her."

I kneel on her other side, reaching for her hand. "Abigail," I whisper. "It's Rissa. I'm right here." I run my other hand down her long braid as Damrion and Adriel rush into the room, their steps thunderous.

"Shit," Damrion growls, assessing the situation in one look. He falls to his knees beside Dax. "What happened?"

"Same as always. She was fine one minute and having a vision the next."

"I was really glad to see you here today," I tell Abigail, tuning Dax and his brothers out. "Um, I was pretty sure that Dax kidnapped me. But I guess he probably didn't if he brought me here. Unless he kidnapped you, too. But you don't strike me as the type who lets herself get kidnapped. You're kind of a badass." I glance up to see Adriel watching me, that one black eye focused on me.

He doesn't seem so hostile now. In fact, when our gazes meet, he inclines his head slightly, something curiously like…gratitude in his expression.

I quickly avert my gaze back to Abigail as a keening cry escapes her lips. She's so pale. Her muscles contort as she thrashes, held down by Dax and Damrion. Whatever she's going through can't be easy. It has to hurt.

Is it always like this?

She's been so happy and full of life since I came downstairs. She speaks of the visions as if they're simply a part of who she is, as if they're a gift. She didn't complain about them. Not even about this part.

Her courage helps me find a little of my own. If she can face this and still find reasons to laugh and smile, then I can face what's coming my way, too. If it means protecting people like her and Dax, I have to face it. I may be a coward at heart, but I'm not heartless. I understand sacrifice. And this secret Fae town hidden deep within the mountains stands in testament to the sacrifices Dax and the Fae have made for a long, long time. Perhaps longer than I'll ever understand.

I'm not convinced I am who they think I am. But so long as I'm here, I'll help. What other choice is there?

Abigail's entire body goes rigid, a scream ripped from deep within her throat.

Tears leak from the corners of my eyes.

Talking to her isn't helping. Holding her down isn't helping either. She's in pain, and that isn't fair to her. Screw fate or destiny or the Gods or whoever decided she should have to carry such a heavy burden.

I squeeze my eyes closed, reaching for...something. I don't know. The same reserve of energy that's gotten me through every hard day in my life. The same one that saved my life the day my father murdered my mom and tried to kill me. I don't know what to call it. Courage? Strength? Determination? Something else? I don't know, but I reach deep, drawing it into me.

It fills me like a dam bursting the gates. Power rushes into me. Rushes through me, sweeping every piece of me along with it.

"Rissa, *nei*!" Dax shouts. "*Nei*!"

His startled cry comes too late.

The power flows down my arm to Abigail, lighting her in a nimbus. As soon as it touches her, I feel what she does. I *see* what she sees. And, oh God, I wish I didn't.

A bloodcurdling scream rips from my lips as the mangled bodies of everyone I know stretch before me in an endless field of death.

Chapter Six

Dax

"You've got to get her off of Abigail," Damrion growls, as if I wasn't already aware of that. Unfortunately, Rissa clings to Abigail's hand as if it's a lifeline, both Valkyrie and Seer screaming as one.

Rissa's emotions beat at me, horror and rage rising in tandem.

They pull an answering rage to the surface in me. It rises hot and fast, ripping through me in a powerful flood. I fight the urge to grasp *Magn*, desperately trying to gain control of the situation before her heightened emotions send us both into a tailspin we can't recover from.

I've never known of a Valkyrie to burn herself out. But I've never seen one burn as hot and bright as Rissa before, either. She's inexperienced, unaware of the power she holds. Gods only know what harm she's capable of bringing down upon herself.

I don't see what she does as I did in the bar, but I feel enough to know whatever vision she and Abigail are locked in isn't good. They blaze like a golden sun, Rissa's Light shining so bright Damrion shields his eyes against it.

"Rissa, *elskan-ljós*, please." I gently try to pry her hand loose from Abigail's, trying desperately not to hurt her. "Please, let go before you hurt yourself."

If she hears me, she doesn't react. Neither does Abigail. They don't move or flinch. They don't respond at all. They just keep screaming, their bodies contorted in pain as Rissa's power amplifies Abigail's one thousandfold. The more power she feeds into Abigail, the more tangled in Abigail's vision they become. It's a spiderweb, one they cannot free themselves from without help.

Forgive me, Valkyrie.

I grit my teeth and grab her wrist, applying pressure to get her to loosen her grip. It's the only choice left. She won't willingly release Abigail. I don't think she can. And I can't compel her to do so. She's resisted every attempt. Her will is forged from steel.

Her hand spasms, loosening for a split second. I move with all the speed of a Fae, hauling her off Abigail. I land on my back on the floor with her partially on top of me. She's limp in my arms, her Light still blazing.

She stops screaming almost immediately. So does Abigail.

"Jesus Christ," Stephan Anderson, one of the Blooded warriors, whispers from the doorway, his piercing eyes wide. I don't know when he arrived, but he's crowded in the kitchen along with Reaper, Malachi, Adriel, and Damrion, gaping at the woman sprawled across my chest. His *imun-laukr* hangs forgotten in his hands. "What the fuck was that?"

"The Light of a Valkyrie," Reaper responds. He's seen horrors that would break most men, but even he looks rattled. "Alone, their Light is fierce. Together, it rivals the Gods. In battle, they were the most formidable weapon the realms ever had. Though, I've never seen one link with a Seer before today."

"Me either," Malachi says, eyeing Rissa with a newfound respect. "I've never seen one so powerful on her own before. Ever."

"There's never been one this powerful," Damrion agrees, carefully checking over Abigail. The girl has fallen still, but she hasn't awoken from her vision. She lies quietly, her face pale.

Rissa still blazes like the sun in my arms, though her Light slowly dims as her fury fades. I sit upright, hauling her into my arms. I keep her close, running my hands through her hair, murmuring to her. Trying to soothe her back to herself.

She's so strong but so new to this. She doesn't understand how dangerous this world can be. I have to protect her better. That's my job as her mate. To protect her. Even from herself when necessary.

"Did she share Abigail's vision?" Malachi demands to know.

"It certainly looked that way," Adriel growls. "As soon as her Light engulfed Abigail, she went to screaming."

Everyone falls silent, processing this. It's a big deal. Abigail has been our only set of eyes for the last few years, but she doesn't always understand what she sees. She's still young, with no frame of reference for the visions the Gods visit upon her. She does the best she can, of course, and we don't fault her for that. But an extra set of eyes? Someone who may understand the things she does not? It's a tempting consideration for my brothers.

"That could be useful," Malachi mutters.

"*Nei*. I won't allow it," I say, finality in my tone.

"Nor will I," Damrion agrees, his tone an even match for mine. "The Valkyrie has no control over her Light. I won't put either of them through that just to give us an advantage."

"We may need it," Reaper argues.

"We've lived without it thus far." Damrion meets his gaze, his unyielding. "We'll continue to do so unless we have no choice. We don't harm those we guard. Not for any reason. And you saw what just happened. They were in pain no Valkyrie or Blooded should ever feel."

Malachi mutters a curse, but he doesn't disagree. He can't. He saw the same thing we did. He knows the visions cause Abigail pain on their own. Amplifying them like Rissa just did only caused her more. We won't do that to either of them willingly.

"Dax."

My gaze flickers to Rissa. Her eyes are open, anger sizzling in their depths. Pain swirls there too. She remembers.

"*Elskan-ljós*," I breathe, relief washing through me in a warm flood. "You're awake."

"Abigail."

"She's well, *bittesmå ljós*."

She nods, pushing herself into an upright position in my arms. She ignores everyone in the room, focused solely on me. "Take me back to Seattle. Right now, Dax."

"Easy, *elskan-ljós*," I say, trying to put her mind at ease. "Easy. Everything is okay."

"Take me back." She scrambles to her feet, her face paling as if every muscle in her body aches. But she doesn't complain. She simply places her hands on her wide hips to glare down at me. "I mean it. I have to go back right now."

She's panicking, what she saw and what just happened pushing her to the edge of what she's willing to handle. I can't blame her for that. This world is brand new to her, and thus far, it hasn't been a walk through the Shining City. But Seattle is the last place she needs to be with Forsaken on the loose.

"*Elskan-ljós...*" I bound to my feet, fully aware that Stephan and my brothers hang onto every word we speak. They watch every move we make. If I can't soothe my Valkyrie, they'll give me nine kinds of hell later.

"You have to take her," Abigail interrupts before I can find an argument to convince her that all is well. "The Forsaken know we have her. They're going to kill everyone she knows one by one until you take her back."

"*Faen*," Malachie breathes.

"Is this what you Foresaw, *ást-meer*?" Damrion asks Abigail, holding out one hand to pull her into a sitting position.

"Yes."

"*Helvete*," Adriel snarls.

No one else says a word. What can we say? Everyone in this room—*nei*, this town—knows the Forsaken will do exactly as Abigail says. Not because she Foresaw it, but because that's the kind of evil they are. They kill without remorse, destroy without compunction. It's in their nature. It's who they are. If killing everyone Rissa knows gets her where they want her, it's precisely what they'll do.

"How do they know that'll get her anywhere?" Stephan asks, his gray eyes clouded as he looks at every warrior in the room.

"How do the Forsaken know anything?" Derision clouds Adriel's voice. "Gods only know what they can do with their dark magics."

"Right," Stephan agrees. "But either they know the Fae have her, or they think she knows who she is. How else would they expect her to know she's the reason her friends are turning up dead?"

He's right. Their plan wouldn't work if she didn't know anything about what was going on. It'd be a waste of their time, no more useful than grabbing any random Blooded from the street and torturing her for information about this place. The Forsaken must know that Rissa knows. Or they must know that we're hiding her. Either way, they're one step ahead. Somehow.

"I think..." Abigail swallows hard, her hands tremoring in her lap. "I don't think my visions come from my Valkyrie blood, at least not completely."

"What are you saying?" Damrion asks.

"The Forsaken know about her," Rissa answers for her. "They've always known about her."

"*Nei*." Adriel's hand slashes through the air, his tone ringing with finality. "*Nei*. They are not responsible for her visions. She is full of Light."

"*Ja*, she is," Damrion growls.

Abigail starts crying quietly, prompting Adriel to crouch beside her and curl one big arm around her shoulders.

"Of course she is," Rissa agrees. "But that doesn't mean they haven't worked out how to manipulate her visions to send things they want you to see. Do you know how the visions work?" Rissa glances at Adriel. "Do you?" She looks to Damrion and then to me. "For all you know, they do. Telling yourself comforting lies won't win this battle. Believe me, I've been there."

What lies has she told herself? What horrors has she seen in her short life? I'm almost afraid to find out, but I need to know. Helping her heal from them will be the key to winning her heart, I'm sure of it.

And I'm not satisfied with merely possessing her soul. I want every corner of this fierce little Valkyrie's heart, too.

"I *saw* what she saw," Rissa continues quietly, fire in her eyes. "I *felt* what she did. If your Gods visited that upon her, then maybe the Light deserves to fall. Because that was pure hell, and she's been enduring it for years. Years!" She spears every single one of us with a hard look. "And each and every one of you has willingly allowed her to do it."

"It's not their fault," Abigail cries. "Don't be mad at them. Please."

"*Nei, ást-meer*," Damrion says, shoving a hand through his hair, his expression troubled. He looks at Abigail and sees a shining Light. Of course he's never considered that her visions may not all flow from the same source. None of us have considered it. "She's right to call us to task. We swore an oath to protect the Valkyrie, not to exploit their Gifts when it suits our purposes. We should have been guarding you better." He blows out a breath. "If she's correct and the Forsaken have been sending some of your visions, we've failed you."

"You didn't," Abigail cries, flinging her arms around the warrior. "You've never failed me, Damrion."

The warrior sighs, not so easily convinced. I can't blame him. Rissa doesn't understand why we do what we do, but she's not entirely wrong. Abigail may be a powerful Seer, but she *is* still human. And a young one at that. We should be guarding her better. Not because we can't afford for the Forsaken to get their hands on her. Not because of what she does for us. But simply because we're the only family she has now.

"Regardless of where the vision originated, we'll be walking into a trap meant for her," Adriel says, nodding at Rissa. "If they want her in Seattle, it's for a reason."

"*Ja*," I agree. I've considered that. But if we don't go, defeat is all but guaranteed because my brave little Valkyrie will never forgive us if we sacrifice the people she loves in their hour of need. She'll never forgive me.

And that possibility is intolerable. I need her trust. It's the only way I'll ever win her heart.

"How do you feel, *elskan-ljós*?" I ask an hour later, setting a stack of clothing on top of the dresser as I step inside the bedroom. I watch warily as Rissa paces back and forth, restless and ill at ease. I don't think she's rested at all since I brought her upstairs. I don't think she's capable of letting herself. Her friends are in danger, and it weighs heavily on her heart.

"Sore." She turns curious blue eyes on me. "Are the visions always like that for her?"

I hesitate, caught between a comforting lie and the truth. "*Nei*," I admit. "When you touched her, you linked with her. It amplified her power."

Her face falls. "I made it worse."

"You didn't know."

"You could have told me." She blows out a breath, pressing her palms to her cheeks. "You should have told me when I was telling all of you off for letting her go through that. You guys just let me tell you off when I was the one really hurting her. *Why?*"

"Because you weren't wrong." I cross toward her, gently tugging her hands away from her face. "We shouldn't be so willing to allow her to endure such pain. There is no honor in it."

"Then why do it?" she asks, searching my face as if she's genuinely curious. There's no judgment in her question, just a genuine desire to understand.

"It's been three hundred years since the Valkyrie last ferried a soul to Helheim, *lyseste ljós*," I murmur, linking our fingers together. "How many do you think have escaped in that time? How many do you think still roam free?"

"Dax," she whispers, her expression stricken. "Are you saying that every person who has died in the last three hundred years is either roaming, waiting to be ferried to the afterlife, or their souls have been taken by the Forsaken?"

"*Ja*, Valkyrie. That's precisely what I'm saying. There is no honor in allowing Abigail to carry the weight she carries. But without her visions, we're blind, fighting an enemy we cannot defeat. And the longer we stumble, the longer every soul in the realms is at risk. We stumbled in the dark for three hundred years, trying to do this task alone, and we didn't come anywhere close. With her, we're able to find the Blooded and gather them close. Because of her, we found you." I bring her fingers to my lips, brushing kisses across her knuckles. "The Light has always demanded a high price for its greatest gifts, but we pay it because we must. Because there is no other way. The Forsaken cannot win."

If there's penance to pay later, we'll pay it. However we must. But we do what we do because we have no choice. Is it fair? *Nei*. Is it right? *Nei*. Someday, we'll prostrate ourselves at Abigail's feet and beg her forgiveness for failing to keep our oath to protect her. But the Gods sent our greatest weapon against the Forsaken when they sent her. And now, through her, they've sent the world's greatest weapon against the dark.

A warrior's life is one of sacrifice. A Fae's life is one of pain. We know both intimately. Our people are gone, *Álfheimr* destroyed. Valhalla lost. And still, we stand. Still, we fight. When the war is done and the dust settles, we settle the bill. It's all we can do.

And that has to be enough.

Rissa blows out a breath. "I'm sorry," she whispers. "I shouldn't have said what I did down there. I didn't understand."

"You did nothing wrong." I release her hand, tucking a strand of hair behind her ear. "As Malachi would say, no harm, no foul."

She rewards me with a tiny smile. "He's an interesting Fae."

"*Ja*. That's one way to put it."

"Are they really your brothers?"

"*Nei*, not in the way you mean. We do not share common lineage. But we are what humans call a troop, a soldier unit. We've trained together since the day we entered Valhalla."

"About that." She pauses. "Um, you're not dead...right?"

It's my turn to smile. I take her hand, placing it over my heart so she can feel the way it thuds for her. "*Nei*, Valkyrie. My heart still beats." I pause. "Or perhaps it beats again."

A soft blush suffuses her cheeks as she lays her palm flat against my chest. "Dax, I..."

"I've spent millennia surrounded by death," I whisper, my voice a scrap of sound. "Sometimes, I wondered if my heart beat at all. I felt half alive for most of that time. That's no longer true."

"S-since you've been on earth?"

"Since you called my soul." I was born for war. It's all I've ever known. The last three hundred years have been the worst for all of us, I think. We've all felt half alive, cut off from everything we know. Waiting for a war we may not win. Living in peace for the first time in our lives. I hated every moment of it. But for the first time ever, peace doesn't sound so bad.

For the first time ever, I wonder what it would be like to simply lay my weapons down and stop fighting. To spend my life devoted to this woman and her care. Every moment I spend with her, some part of me craves it a little more.

More than our return to Valhalla or an end to the Forsaken and the threat of the dark...I want a future with her. I want her in my arms and in my bed.

"Kiss me, Dax," she pleads quietly. "Kiss me like you did this morning."

I drag her into my arms with a guttural groan, incapable of denying her. My soul is hers, bound to her in every way.

There is nothing I wouldn't give her if she asked it of me. No law I would not break, no sin I would not commit.

"Valkyrie," I breathe, my lips inches from hers as I cradle her head in my hand. *"Jeg lengter etter deg."* It's nothing but the truth. I long for her in ways I cannot put into words. It's soul hunger, wild and fierce. I don't know how to contain it. No Fae has ever had to try. It's been two thousand years since a Fae last took a mate, and one has never laid claim to a Guardian of Valhalla's soul. The old ways no longer apply. They died with *Álfheimr*.

We make our own rules now.

I brush my lips across Rissa's in soft passes, drawing her closer to me. Her soft body presses against my chest, her warmth searing me. Even now, her power hasn't faded entirely. Her Light still swirls around her, radiant and bright. Everywhere it touches, I tremble, aching for her. Gods, how I ache.

Her lips part on a soft sigh, her eyelids fluttering closed.

"Open your eyes, *elskan-ljós*." I don't want her hiding from me. When I kiss her, I want her to know it's me. I want those blue eyes locked with mine, staring into my soul.

Her sooty lashes flutter against her alabaster skin. She opens them slowly, focusing on me. Desire swirls through the depths of her eyes, turning the bright blue to dark midnight. I reflect back like a field of stars, painted across her irises.

"Beautiful." I drape her over my arm, nuzzling my face into her throat, breathing her in. Even dressed in one of my shirts and a pair of borrowed sweats, she smells the same, like a field of wildflowers. Even here, where snow clings to the ground well past its time, those grow wherever they find a patch of sun. They're hardy little things, stretching boldly toward the sky as if unafraid of the inevitable frost.

She reminds me of them. Beautiful, wild, growing where she's planted, no matter what stands in her way. She is no coward, despite what she thinks. She's fierce and bright, a Valkyrie to her core.

"Dax," she moans, clinging to my shoulders as I kiss a trail down her throat. My tongue dips into the hollow of her collarbone, tasting her there. She's delicious, sweet and salty perfection. I quest lower, running my tongue along the teasing bit of cleavage her modest little top reveals.

She arches toward my mouth, sighing.

I can't resist covering one full breast with my palm.

"Oh," she whispers, her eyes wide open.

I pinch the hard bud of her nipple between my thumb and forefinger, exploring. Experimenting. Learning what she likes. She definitely likes that. She gasps my name, her nails digging into my shoulders.

Her light flares brighter, searing me with her desire. It mixes with mine, wresting what little control I have out of my hands. I growl, dragging the top of her shirt down. Her bra tugs against her nipple before that hard little bud pops free.

My teeth close around it, pulling it deep into my mouth.

"Dax!" Her hand flies to the back of my head, holding me there. Not that I need the encouragement. She tastes like sugar, that addictive substance humans add to everything. I never understood the appeal until this very moment. *Ja.* I could glut myself on this woman's taste every day.

I bite and suck her nipple, driving us both into a frenzy. Gods. I need more. *Nei.* I need her, stripped bare and dripping around my fingers. Maybe then I'll be able to think straight. Maybe then I'll be able to breathe through the furious need churning through my veins.

Or maybe I won't. Maybe nothing short of fucking my way into this Valkyrie's soul and taking up permanent residence in every corner will satisfy me. *Ja.* That sounds good.

I back her toward the bed, one implacable step at a time.

"W-what are you doing?"

"Showing you what it means to bind the soul of a Fae, little Valkyrie," I purr, toppling her to the bed. She lands on her back, her mass of hair fanning around her. I reach over my head, dragging my shirt off. I want her hands on me, too. Gods. I need to feel her skin-to-skin.

Her eyes widen as they fall upon my body, her tongue dancing along her bottom lip. She reaches out, pausing with her fingers half an inch from my abdomen. I crawl on top of her, straddling her legs.

"Touch me, *elskan-ljós*," I growl. "Put your hands on my flesh."

She doesn't have to be told twice. She immediately sits up beneath me, placing one palm flat against my chest. The other she uses to balance herself.

I groan, my head falling back as her Light pours over me, turning my cock to steel. Ah, Gods. Pure power flows from her into me, setting me aflame. I burn like the brightest star, caught tightly in her net.

"You're so beautiful, Adaxiel." She runs her hand across my chest and then down, feeling every ridge of my abdomen, exploring every inch of skin. "I didn't know a warrior could be so perfect."

Gods, she's killing me.

Her hand drifts lower.

I capture it with mine, pushing her gently to her back. If she explores any lower, we won't be going to Seattle today or any other day. She won't be leaving this bed at all.

I capture her hands in mine, holding them hostage as I kiss her again, hard and deep. She fights to free herself before giving up with a displeased little grunt. The sound makes me smile. My little Valkyrie doesn't like being bossed. She doesn't like ceding control. That's all right. She'll learn that outside of this room, I'm hers to command. But in this bed, my word is law.

I adjust my hold on her hands, containing them both in one of mine. I use the other to touch her everywhere. She's so much softer than I am, so much sweeter. Every inch of her is sweet perfection. I can't wait to unveil every inch and worship on my knees.

Regrettably, it's a dream I won't get to bring to life today. If I get her clothes off her now, there will be no stopping. My control is already in tatters around me. I'm stripped raw, clinging to honor by the skin of my teeth, and she's not ready yet. Not for what I want. Not for what it means for both of us.

But that doesn't mean I can't give her the taste she craves.

"Do you want to come, *elskan-ljós*?" I breathe against her throat, running my hand up and down her thigh. "Do you want to know what it's like to let this Fae love you?"

"I...I've never..."

"*Ja*, I know."

"I'm afraid," she whispers.

My heart threatens to tear itself into shreds. "Of me?"

"Of myself. Of us." She swallows. "Of l-love. In my world, love is pain, Dax. It hurts so damn bad."

"Not any longer, Valkyrie," I vow, brushing my lips across hers. "Not with me. My soul is bound to yours. Any hurt you suffer, I suffer too. Any pain you feel, I feel, too. I'll let the realms fall to Darkness before I allow you to come to harm. That's my oath to you."

Her eyes flit across my face. "You mean that, don't you?"

"Every word."

She watches me for a moment, drawing her courage around her. And then she nods, so much braver than she has any right to be after everything she's endured since the Forsaken found her in the bar. Gods. Whatever life she lived before, she must have been fierce. "Then show me what it means to let a Fae love me, Dax. Show me what it means to let you love me."

I groan, pressing my face to her throat as an endless well of gratitude pours through me. I send up a silent prayer, something I haven't done in two thousand years...not since Freyr died on the battlefield and *Álfheimr* fell.

Tyr, give me strength to defend her. Odin, grant me the wisdom to guide her. Freyr, give me the Light to shine upon her path. Freya, teach me the patience needed to love her carefully. Do not let me fail her.

I drag my hand up her thigh, kissing my way down her chest at the same time. My lips close around her nipple as I slip my hand beneath the waistband of her pants. She gasps, her back bowing from the bed.

Her sweet sounds spur me on. I lick and bite, stroking my fingers against her mound, teasing her. She shifts restlessly beneath me, eager for something she doesn't yet understand. She will soon.

When I can't stand it any longer, I slip my hand lower. My cock presses against my zipper, a desperate growl crawling up my throat. She's hot, wet silk against my fingertips, burning hot. Ah, Gods. She's so eager, so ready. *So wet.*

I run my thumb along her bare slit, unsure if I have the control for this. *Nei*. I'll find the control for this. For her, I'll move mountains if that's what the bond demands of me. Whatever it takes to prove to this fierce little warrior that she's safe in my hands in every way, every day.

"Rissa, Valkyrie," I groan against her breast. "You're the sweetest silk."

"Dax, please!"

"What do you need, *lyseste ljós*?"

"You!"

"You have me." I nip her skin, exploring every inch of her folds, fascinated by the way she trembles beneath me.

I feel her again, like a little ball of living sensation in the corner of my mind. It quivers and expands with every caress. I can't see what she does, can't read her mind. But her pleasure feeds mine, creating a harmonic that sends fingers of sensation dancing up my spine.

Gods. How much more powerful will it be when she allows me into her soul? When she accepts the bond between us and forges a bridge between us that nothing and no one will ever be able to destroy? There will be no keeping me out then. I'll know exactly how she feels at every moment, and she'll know the same.

I press my thumb to the little bundle of nerves begging for my attention. She gasps, her Light blazing bright as a sun again. It engulfs me in a crackling nimbus, lighting me up from the inside out. My own power rises hot and swift in response, surging through me in a flood.

It pours into Rissa, pulling a cry from her lips. "Dax!"

I try to pull back, thinking she's afraid, but before I can move, she digs her nails into my back.

"Please," she cries. "Oh, God, please."

Only then do I realize it isn't fear pouring from her. It's pleasure so intense it borders on pain. She isn't frightened by my power or the intensity of my desire. She revels in it like a cat bathing in the sun.

Somehow, this mysterious little Valkyrie, who doesn't even understand the power she wields, let alone know how to control it, figures out how to use it to draw more of mine into her. She drinks from me again and again, filling herself so full of Fae power the entire room burns bright.

"Now, let it pop like a balloon," I growl, grinding my thumb against that bundle of nerves. "Let it spill over you, Valkyrie."

She fumbles, trying to sort out how to do that. I don't offer instructions. She got this far on her own. She can figure this part out, too. It's instinct with her.

It doesn't take her long to figure out how to do this part, either. Within moments, she's figured out how to do what I demand. I don't warn her what's about to happen. If she wants to play with Fae power, she's going to get burned.

She lets the well inside of her pop. A tidal wave of sensation roars through her—every single thing I feel hitting her in a shockwave of emotion. She gasps, her eyes going wide as fierce desire and piercing need rip through her.

"Please," she gasps, her voice strangled. She writhes beneath me, caught in a web of her own making.

I take pity on her, grinding my thumb against her clit again and again as she shakes and moans and pleads, her eyes wild with desire. Now she understands what it's like to be loved by a Fae. We aren't gentle creatures. We're warriors of the Light. We love as hard as we fight...with every ounce of our souls.

I've held myself in check, keeping a tight leash on myself, simply because it was what she needed from me. No more.

She will always be safe with me because I'll destroy entire worlds to ensure it. That's the Fae way. And that's the power we wield. It's wild and fierce, as much a part of the Fae as the Fae who wields it. I wield mine for her now. Since the moment she called my soul, I've belonged to her.

She shatters in my arms, her Light growing as bright as a supernova. As she falls apart, writhing and gasping my name, her Light finally begins to dim, drained for once. Perhaps this Valkyrie is more like the Fae than expected. Emotion fuels her, feeding her power. She reaches for it when she feels anything deeply. It's instinctive to her, as instinctive as it is to a Fae.

Instinct, I understand. The symbiotic relationship between emotion and power is one every Fae knows. This is a good sign. Perhaps we aren't so helpless when it comes to training this Valkyrie after all.

She trembles a final time and then falls still.

I scoop her into my arm, holding her close to my heart. My lips run across her forehead, words of praise falling from them. She doesn't rest for long.

Within moments, her eyes pop open, focusing on me. "What was that?"

"That's Fae power, Valkyrie," I purr against her skin. "Our power is part of the Fae who wields it. Everything we feel feeds it, fueling it."

She processes that for a moment. "So had you been very angry?"

"A wave of fury would have rolled over you, so intense you would have felt your blood boil in your veins."

"Well, then," she whispers. "I guess it's a good thing you weren't very mad, wasn't it?"

"At you?" I tip her chin up, smiling. "Never, Valkyrie."

She blushes, averting her gaze. "Um, do you always feel…that?"

"For you? Always."

"Oh." She swallows. "Um, is it always like that? So…intense?"

"I wouldn't know. I've never been mated. And no Fae warrior has ever been soul-bound to a Valkyrie."

Her gaze flies to mine, shock written all over her face. "Never? As in never-ever?"

"Never-ever. We're the first, *lyseste ljós*."

"How? Why?"

"Odin forbade it. The Fae were meant to guard all the Valkyrie and Valhalla. We couldn't fulfill that oath if our loyalties were to the one Valkyrie that held our bond."

"You couldn't do both?"

"*Nei*. We aren't designed that way, *bittesmå ljós*. Once you claim a Fae's soul, his loyalty is to you and you alone, as it should be."

"As it should be?" She stares at me like I've lost my mind. And then some thought occurs to her. One that has her sitting upright, horror dawning in her eyes. "Dax...if I fall to the Dark, what happens to you?"

This is one question I don't want to answer. But I won't lie to her. I can't, not if I'm ever going to gain her trust. "There's a reason so many Valkyrie died in battle, Rissa," I say quietly. "When their bonded warriors fell beneath the might of the enemy, so did they. Once a bond is complete, there is no surviving. If one falls, they both fall."

"That's...barbaric," Rissa whispers in horror.

"Perhaps, but you can't live with half a soul. The warriors granted a second life knew this. They accepted it. So did the Valkyrie. Every great gift demands a price. That's always been the cost of power." I brush my lips across her forehead before dragging myself from the bed. "It's what holds us to the Light and keeps us from falling to the dark. The Forsaken pay no such price for their power."

"There has to be a better way."

"Perhaps." I shrug, gently kissing her forehead. "Or perhaps this is the most compassionate way. I spent millennia with the Valkyries and the warriors, Rissa. Not a single one would have willingly chosen to survive the death of his or her bonded mate. Not one."

She nods, her brow furrowed as if she's deep in thought.

"I need to go check in with Damrion. Why don't you shower and get dressed? We'll be leaving soon."

She doesn't respond, her mind a million miles away.

I watch her for a long moment before sighing quietly and slipping from the room. Perhaps she's right and the price of the bond is too high. I don't know. But I do know one thing. If she were to fall to the Dark, my death would be a mercy. I wouldn't want to survive it.

She means too much already.

Chapter Seven

Rissa

"Rissa! Rissa, wait!" Abigail comes flying out of a small cabin, her braid flying behind her as she races down the sidewalk toward me, arms flailing over her head.

I pause, waiting for her to catch up to me.

She stumbles to a stop, her boots sinking deep into the snow at our feet. Her breath steams before her as she pants. The temperature plummeted as soon as the sun dipped below the horizon. The final rays still linger, still fighting for dominion this far west. But shadows have already begun to overtake Eitr, turning the Fae stronghold into a frigid, frozen relic from an age long since passed. If that age ever dawned at all in this world.

Eitr is like no town I've ever seen before. Every building looks as if it sprang from the ground, fully formed. They don't mimic nature, they're built to be part of it, blending seamlessly with the dense forest growing right up around it. You could stumble up to the gates of the massive wall encircling the town and not even realize you were there. It's impressive, clearly designed to stay hidden...and even more clearly designed for defense.

Seeing it from the window was one thing. Seeing it from the ground is another. The wall itself is nearly as tall as the trees that buttress it, every log carefully placed. So was every building, I think. Their placement carefully and skillfully chosen. Larger homes like Dax's ring the perimeter, serving almost as an inner wall. Smaller homes—adorable little cabins that seem designed more for comfort than utility like the others—twist and turn along paths in front of the larger dwellings. Every path leads toward the heart of Eitr, the domed spire of the Hall at the center. Smaller buildings flank the Hall—shops and the like, I assume.

The Hall is clearly the heart of the town, though. It shines at the center.

"We have to visit the Hall before you leave," Abigail says as if reading what's in my mind.

I glance up at her, startled. She's an unusual girl, far more perceptive than anyone I've ever met. She's so full of life, shining brightly, but she's wise beyond her years. I can't imagine living with the burden she's carried for so long. It has to be exhausting, yet she carries it as if it's easy.

"Why?" I ask.

Her brows furrow, her gaze turning uncertain. "I don't know. I just know that we have to visit the Hall before you leave. You have to see something inside."

I turn to look for Dax, who is further up the sidewalk, talking to the group of warriors accompanying us back to Seattle. Damrion, Adriel, Malachi, and Reaper are all going. So is Stephan, and a human named Garrison who looks mean enough to command giants. Ten additional Fae will also accompany us, but I can't remember their names. I barely remember their faces.

It's been a long, long day.

I catch Dax's gaze and motion for him.

He murmurs something to Damrion. The two warriors break away from the group and jog back to us.

"What's wrong, Valkyrie?" Dax asks, reaching for my hand as soon as he's near.

"I'm not sure." I frown up at him. "Abigail says I have to visit the Hall before I leave. I need to see something there."

Damrion looks to Abigail, his lips pursed. "Can it not wait, *ást-meer*? The mountain will be treacherous in the dark."

"No," she says, her shoulders back and her chin firmed as if she's preparing for battle. "It's important, Damrion. She has to go now. Before she leaves."

"Another vision?" Dax asks her.

"I..." She presses her fingertips to her temples. "I don't know. I can't remember. But if she doesn't go, something bad is going to happen. I feel it."

"Easy, *ást-meer*. We'll take her," Damrion says, instantly solicitous.

Relief falls over Abigail's face. The four of us turn to make the trek toward the Hall.

"Where are you going?" Reaper shouts.

"Prepare to leave!" Damrion shouts back. "We have something to take of before we go."

The warriors murmur behind us, but they don't ask any questions. They don't complain, either. I think Damrion might be their leader. At least to some extent. They respect his orders when he issues them.

I watch him from the corner of my eye as we walk, curious about him. He's quiet compared to the other Fae—at least compared to Reaper and Malachi. He seems more...reserved, less as if his emotions rule him.

"What are you thinking, Valkyrie?" Dax murmurs, his lips close to my ear.

"About Damrion."

Dax growls, pulling me to a stop. His green eyes narrow on me, strong emotion swirling through them. "Do you want to try that again, *bittesmå ljós*?"

I gape at him, caught off guard. Is he jealous? Oh, my goodness. He *is* jealous!

"I didn't mean it like that, Dax." I roll my eyes at him even as my heart flutters. He's an ancient Fae warrior, more fierce and beautiful than anyone I've ever met in my life. But he's jealous over me. I shouldn't encourage that. I shouldn't like it. Yet, I do.

I felt his emotions for me in the bedroom today. They rolled over me like a heatwave, branding him on my soul. This Fae is going to change my life. He's going to change everything.

"Explain," he rumbles, still not appeased.

"He seems different than your brothers," I explain. "More reserved. There's almost something…calming about him. I'm not sure I'm explaining it right."

Dax's expression clears. "He's *konunga-kyn*, royal kin."

"Royal kin? You mean he's royalty?"

"*Ja*. His *langamma*, grandmother, was Fjölnir's daughter."

"I don't know the name," I admit.

"Fjölnir was Freyr and Gerðr's son. Freyr was one of the Vanir who rules over *Álfheimr*."

"Oh." I glance at Damrion, who has continued down the path with Abigail. He looks the same as he did two minutes ago. "It's hard to wrap my mind around the fact that you walked with Gods," I admit. "To me, they're just stories everyone knows. But you really knew them. Damrion is related to one of them."

"Come." He tugs gently on my hand to get me moving again. "Humans have an odd way of looking at Gods," he says as we walk, snow crunching beneath our feet. "To you, they're beings who can do no wrong. You revere and fear them, placing them on pedestals. It wasn't always that way. In most of the realms, Gods were just the race that ruled over us. They weren't without faults and flaws. They weren't all good or all bad. They just were."

"I know," I admit. "Those stories survived. But trying to reconcile the fact that the stories were real is still a lot. Like a *lot*." I risk a glance up at him. "Religion is a touchy subject for humans. It's the one thing I think we're still willing to die for. If the world knew we got it wrong..."

"Who says you're wrong?" He cocks a brow at me. "The Æsir died two thousand years ago, *elskan-ljós*. No one knows who took their place. Maybe your Christian God.

Maybe the Muslims' Allah. Maybe some God no one has yet named."

"You believe there's still a God out there somewhere?" I ask, shocked.

"Perhaps, perhaps not. But many of your people believe, and that belief holds them to the Light." He smiles at me, a charming, crooked smile. "It provides hope. That's a powerful thing, Valkyrie."

I nod my agreement as we pass beyond the final cabin, stepping out onto the town square. The Hall looms up ahead, standing higher than any other building in town. It's beautiful, a true work of art, like the cathedrals of old. Only this one is carved entirely of wood, each ornate design painstakingly crafted by hand.

"It's beautiful," I whisper.

"We lost sixty-nine Fae when the portal collapsed. And hundreds more on the other side," he says softly, leading me up the steps. "This is a place of honor for our dead."

Damrion and Abigail wait for us outside the doors.

"We should wait out here," Abigail announces when we reach them. "They need to go in alone."

Damrion frowns, but he doesn't gainsay her. I don't think the kindhearted Fae has it in him to tell the little human no.

Dax reaches for an ornately carved handle, pulling open the door.

I step through with him following behind.

I feel him calling his power to him. It washes over me as his *lyststål* appears in his hands, acting like a light to guide our way. I gasp when he holds it aloft, and my gaze falls on the walls. An entire history spills across the wood in vivid color, painstakingly painted across every inch of space. *Yggdrasil* stands at the center, its branches burning.

"Dax," I whisper. "What is this?"

"Our history, *elskan-ljós*. The history of the Fae."

I turn in a circle, my heart rising and falling. *Álfheimr* stretches across one entire wall, standing in testament to the beauty of the realm. It's like Earth, with its forests, rivers, and lakes. Only it's somehow far more beautiful. Fae cities rise from the forest, standing like sentinels among the trees, strong and proud. A couple wearing beautiful golden crowns adorned with massive jewels watch over the realm, surrounded by flows of Light. It's peaceful, beautiful. A realm of tranquility.

But thousands of Fae leave anyway, long lines marching toward another realm. *Valhalla*. They ring a city of gold, fearsome expressions on their faces as they stand guard over the city. Beautiful women fly in and out, surrounded by blazing light. Some Fae teach human men to fight.

Others accompany the Valkyrie as they carry orbs of light toward a glowing doorway.

My gaze falls on the next wall.

Ragnarök and the fall of *Álfheimr*. Tears well in my eyes at the sight of so many Fae lying still on a battlefield, their realm burning around them. In the sky overhead, a Giant battles the same man from the previous wall, both bleeding. I turn slightly and see the God on his knees, falling to his death. The Giant falls, too. The entire realm burns to ash, leaving nothing behind... nothing except a battalion of Fae, fighting in Valhalla.

Valkyrie and warriors litter the ground. Others glow like little suns, setting fire to Giants. The Fae battle on, unleashing their rage upon the enemy. Valhalla is overrun with enemies. They outnumber the Fae and the Valkyrie by hundreds. But the Fae battle on.

I turn slowly, watching as the tide of the battle turns and the Fae gain the upper hand, driven by their grief and rage and the oath that bound them. They don't falter. They don't flee. They fight, protecting this realm as they couldn't their own.

Somehow, they drive out the invaders. They bury their dead and rebuild. There are far fewer Valkyrie pictured now. Far fewer Fae, too. But still, the Fae battle on. Valkyrie after Valkyrie shows up pregnant, their bellies swollen.

Tears flow freely as the Valkyrie place their infants in baskets and leave them behind, hiding them on Earth where the Forsaken won't find them. The grief etched onto their faces breaks me. I cover my mouth with my hand and sob. Those poor women. They gave up everything, including their own children, just to give the realms a chance.

This is the silent burden the Fae carry. The memories they'll never forget. And there are so many more of them. So many moments of heartbreak, of devastating loss, etched into the walls of this hall so they never forget what they've lost and what they fight for even now.

The Valkyrie aren't the brightest Lights the realms have. The Fae are. They always have been.

I turn to Dax, tears pouring down my cheeks, and fling myself at the hard wall of his chest. "I'm sorry," I whisper, clinging to his broad shoulders. "I'm so sorry, Dax."

"Shh, Valkyrie. All is well."

It isn't, though. It's not even close.

Once I stop crying, Dax leads me around the Hall. I'm not sure precisely what I was supposed to see here. But I make sure I look at everything, committing the images to memory.

"Who painted this, Dax?" I ask.

"Adriel," he murmurs.

"He's incredibly skilled."

"*Ja*, he is."

I draw to a stop in front of the last wall. This one shows the fall of Valhalla three hundred years ago. Unlike the others, hundreds of names are swirled into the paint, as if each stroke of color spells a piece of that Fae's story.

I reach out, gently tracing my fingers along one of the names. *Druxien.*

"Are these the Fae who died?"

"*Ja*. And the Valkyrie and warriors." His stoic expression breaks my heart. "Everyone the Fae lost during the fall of Valhalla is recorded here."

"I'm sorry, Dax."

"As am I, *bittesmå ljós*." He lifts my hand to his lips, brushing a kiss across my knuckles as if to soothe me, even though he's the one who lost so much.

We stand in silence for a long moment before I feel compelled to speak again. "My father was an abusive alcoholic," I whisper. "Um, he'd drink a lot and get really violent. My mom tried to protect me as much as she could. When I was nine, he got really bad. She decided to take me and run."

"Rissa," Dax breathes.

"He came home while she was packing our stuff." I squeeze my eyes closed, only to pop them open wide again immediately when memories of that night flicker against the backs of my eyelids. "Um, as soon as he realized what was happening, he flew into a rage. He started screaming that we weren't leaving him, that we were never leaving him." My hands shake as I share my own painful history with the Fae who has lived through so much pain. "He killed my mom. He tried to kill me. I think he would have succeeded if the neighbors hadn't heard all of the noise and called the police."

"*Faen*," Dax growls, his *lyststål* flaring with power. Rage swirls like thunderclouds in his eyes, his expression savage. "Your own father tried to kill you, *elskan-ljós*? Your own father?"

"Yes."

"*Where is he?*" The lethal menace in his voice sends a chill down my spine. I think he'd rip my father apart piece by piece and enjoy every minute of it if he could get his hands on him. He'd dance in a shower of his blood with a smile on his face and not feel a second of remorse or regret. For me, he'd forsake the Light in a quest for revenge.

Fear rips through me, understanding dawning. I know why Abigail sent me here, what I had to see. I know what I need to do now. *Protect Dax.*

For the first time since meeting him, I lie.

"He's in prison," I say, glancing down at my hands. "He'll be there for the rest of his life." It's not true. He was released almost two years ago. He spent less time in prison for murder than some people spend for drug crimes. Our system is broken. But I can't tell Dax that now.

Not with Abigail's vision still fresh in my mind. My friends' bodies weren't the only ones piled before us in an endless field of death. So was my father's.

The Forsaken have him.

And I don't know what I'm supposed to do about that.

I know what Dax would do, though. Dax would let him die or find a way to ensure his death.

I've never forgiven my father for what he did. But I've never been able to stop loving him, either. That's my big secret. That's the pain I carry. My father tried to kill me...and some part of me loves him still.

How am I supposed to confess that to the man who would forsake the Light to avenge me? I can't.

"Kiss me, Dax," I plead instead. "Please, kiss me and tell me everything will work out."

"*Ja,*" he growls, releasing his *lyststål* to draw me into his arm. The Hall is plunged into darkness, the only light trickling in from the dome overhead. Moonlight spills down over us as he presses me back against the wall, his warrior's body blocking out the entire world. His lips come down on mine, his kiss tinged with the weight of his emotions, as if they trickle out, too strong to be contained.

They sear me, burning away the chill clinging to me, the one that goes soul-deep. Hunger rises swiftly in a tidal wave so much larger than anything I've ever felt before. I cling to Dax, desperate to drown in it...in him. In the way he makes me feel so much, so easily. I should be terrified of that, but more and more, I find myself eagerly reaching for it, desperately grasping for the sense of rightness I feel whenever he's nearby.

"Gods," he groans, breaking the kiss to drag his lips down my throat. "I kiss you and forget the dark exists, Valkyrie."

"Me too." I pull his hair, silently asking for more. Of his kisses. Of his Light. Of whatever he's willing to give me.

He nuzzles his face between my breasts, breathing deeply. His hands move over me, scorching me alive. "I need one more taste, Rissa. Just one more before we go."

"Yes," I whisper without hesitation. "Please, yes."

He slips his hands into my pants without another word, too impatient to wait. That makes two of us. I've been dying for his touch since the moment he released me in his room. I gasp, gripping his hair in my hands as he immediately slips one hand between my thighs. I'm wet for him already, soaked, really.

He feels it for himself and growls, slipping my panties to the side.

I come up on my toes, trying to stifle a cry of ecstasy as his wicked fingers immediately set to work. His hand moves in a blur, his skillful fingers dancing over every sensitive place he learned earlier. He nips and kisses my throat, my chest, my lips, whispering sweet words as he drives me higher, right there against the wall, the history of the Fae surrounding us.

I crack apart with a sharp cry of relief, shattering into a million tiny pieces in his arms.

He strokes me through it, murmuring to me, and then sweetly, gently puts me back together again.

When he's done, he's stolen the biggest pieces of my heart, claiming them for himself. And I'm less sure than ever that I deserve him.

Chapter Eight

Rissa

The drive down the mountain is every bit as treacherous as Damrion promised. I nestle in Dax's arms in the back of Malachi's truck, alternately gripping the door handle for dear life, and trying desperately to distract myself from my thoughts.

The truck slips and slides on patches of black ice, not even the chains helping much. Malachi is more serious than I've ever seen him, all of his attention focused on the road. Reaper sits beside him in the front seat, his eyes focused on the roadway too.

"Close your eyes, Rissa," Dax murmurs. "Relax."

"Easy for you to say. I'm not entirely sure an accident would kill anyone else in this truck," I mutter, eyeing him sideways. "But if we go over the side of the mountain, it'll definitely take me out."

"Malachi won't allow us to go over the side." Dax smiles. "He doesn't suck as a driver."

"I heard that," Malachi says. "I'm fucking excellent behind the wheel."

I smile despite myself. The giant warrior is like a big kid. He doesn't take anything seriously for long.

"You need sleep."

"I'm not very tired."

"You are." Dax runs his lips across my forehead. "Close your eyes, *bittesmå ljós*. I'll hold you while you sleep."

"What about you?" I eye him suspiciously. "Fae do sleep, right?" If they do, he certainly hasn't done much of it.

"*Ja*." A smile dances across his lips, his eyes haunting in the pale moonlight. "Fae sleep, Valkyrie."

"Just checking." I lay my head against his chest with a sigh. "You might as well tell me how this Valkyrie power works, Dax. If I'm supposed to use it, I'm going to have to know how."

"You already know how," he says. "You wield it like the Fae wield *Magn*. It's an instinct for you, something you reach for when you feel something deeply. You've probably been grasping for it your entire life and just didn't know it."

"Wouldn't someone have noticed?"

"Humans don't notice most things that are right under their noses. They're oblivious," he says, running his hands through my hair. When his fingers catch on tangles, he sets to work gently unsnarling them. "And they have no aptitude for magic. At most, they'd have noticed a glow, but nothing more."

"Wouldn't *I* have noticed?" I ask, my voice whisper soft.

His hands still in my hair. "A Valkyrie doesn't reach her full power until adulthood, *bittesmå ljós*. You would have been using only small amounts of your power until recently. Perhaps not even enough for you to understand what you were doing."

Have I been using this Light my entire life? I think back, remembering all the times I was overwhelmed by emotion. Every time, I reached deep into that well inside, grasping for some hidden reserve I never understood. I told myself it was strength or courage, whatever I needed in the moment to face whatever stood in my path. Without fail, I reached for it. And without fail, I faced what came. I won battles I shouldn't have won, faced bullies who simply decided to walk away. I survived my father when I should have died.

I never understood exactly why he stopped hurting me that night. He just...lit up like lightning and quit. Did I make him quit? Was I the reason he lit up like that? I've been shying away from those answers for days, hesitant to revisit that night. But I think I was. I think *I* stopped him.

Was that this power all along? Is that what got me through every hard day? Every impossible situation?

I think so. And if that was only a fraction of it...if what I did to that Forsaken at the bar or what happened with Abigail is only a fraction of what I can do, what are the true limits to the well within me?

I'm almost afraid to find out.

"So Valkyrie don't reach power until they're fully grown? They grow up normal?"

Dax hesitates.

"The Valkyrie weren't a race, Rissa. Once, they were human or Fae or Giant or Dwarf. They were called to serve because they felt a connection to the dead," Reaper says from the front seat, alerting me to the fact that he and Malachi are listening to our conversation. "They were the special few who could cradle the souls of the dead in the palms of their hands."

"Oh." I process this, trying to shift it into place in my mind. There's so much about this world I don't understand, so much about it that's completely at odds with the stories my mom told me. And yet so much of what she told me never felt quite right to me, either. There's a sense of rightness to this piece.

"Um, did the Valkyrie ever see things that no one else saw? Or hear things no one else heard?" I ask, my voice soft.

"Perhaps," Malachi says gently. "The Valkyrie never spoke much about their experiences with the souls of the dead. To them, their stewardship over the dead was sacred, something shared only between Valkyrie. But *ja*, I imagine they did hear them crying out. I imagine they may have even seen them passing over."

Dax continues running his hands through my hair, not speaking. None of them ask me if I see or hear things that aren't there. Either they don't want to know, or they respect the Valkyrie's stewardship over souls too much even now to ask. But for the first time in my life, I consider the possibility that maybe, just maybe, I'm not crazy. Maybe, like the ancestor who placed her infant in a basket and hid her on Earth, the things I've seen and heard my whole life have been the souls of the dead crying out to me, trying to capture my attention.

I've spent so much of my life afraid of them. Instead, I should have been weeping for them. Because there was nowhere for them to go. For three hundred years, there has been no afterlife waiting. There's just been that void in between...that infernal place before the Veil where souls once went to wait, but now go to die. The place where the

Forsaken stalk them through the dark, picking them off one by one.

Is my mom's soul still floating free out there?

"How do I ferry souls across?" I ask.

"You don't," Dax says, a note of finality in his voice.

"But I'm a Valkyrie, Dax. Isn't that my job? To help ferry them across the Veil to the afterlife?"

"*Nei*." He clenches his jaw, glancing away from me.

Malachi and Reaper say nothing.

I stare at Dax, trying to sort out why he's suddenly so closed off and rigid, and then realization dawns. "You're afraid to let me try," I guess. "You think I can't do it."

"*Nei, lyseste ljós*," he growls. "I think you will do exactly what you set out to do. You'll figure out precisely how to get across the Veil with as many souls as you can carry. And as soon as you do, you'll walk right into whatever trap the Forsaken set for you. Your Light will fall into their hands, and there will be nothing we can do to stop it." He glowers at me, a specter in the dark. "I forbid it."

"You can't forbid me from doing anything, Dax. If I'm a Valkyrie, this is what I'm supposed to do. It's what I was put here to do!"

"*Nei*," he growls. "You were put here to save souls, not to risk your own on a fool's errand."

"Then I guess it's a good thing that it's not up to—"

Static crackles through the truck from the walkie-talkie situated in the console. Half a second later, one of the warriors shout into it. "Forsaken! There are Forsaken in the valley!"

"*Faen!*" Dax roars.

Malachi slams on the brakes. The truck fishtails wildly, refusing to stop. For a long moment, I think we're going over the side of the mountain. But at the last second, Malachi manages to whip the wheel. We slide off the road onto a gravel path.

Shouts come through the walkie-talkie, instructions and orders shouted too rapidly for me to understand all of them. I don't even understand half of them. They're a mix of English and the Nordic languages Dax and the Fae speak as easily as they breathe.

Howls rip through the night, one after another after another. They seem to come from everywhere and nowhere at once, echoing off the mountainside. The chilling sound freezes the blood in my veins. Wolves. Dozens of them, from the sounds of it.

"*Varulv,*" Reaper says. "They brought the *varulv.*"

"*Ja,*" Dax says. "They're all over the mountainside."

"What do you want to do, Dax?" Malachi asks.

"Where does this road lead?"

"Down the mountain and around the edges of the valley before linking back up with the highway." Malachi pauses. "It's going to be a rough trip if we take it. It's little more than a cart track in places. We'll have to melt ice to get through."

"Then we melt ice," Dax says. "We can't risk leading them to Eitr, and we can't drive her into an army of Forsaken."

Malachi meets his gaze in the rearview and nods. "Then we continue forward."

"Tighten your belt, Valkyrie," Dax orders. "And stay low. If you see something moving, say something. Understood?"

"Understood."

Malachi inches the truck forward.

Reaper grabs the walkie-talkie. "Damrion."

"I'm here," Damrion answers a moment later.

"There are *varulv* all over the mountainside."

"I heard."

"We're going to attempt to go around the valley."

"Be careful," Damrion orders. "We'll deal with the Forsaken and any *varulv* we come across."

"What are *varulv*? Wolves?"

"Once, they were men. Now, they're more like hellhounds," Reaper says, his tone grim. "A bite by one is fatal, even to a Fae."

"Werewolves. You're talking about werewolves?" Why does my voice sound like that?

"*Nei*, Rissa. Werewolves retain some semblance of their humanity, even when they turn. A *varulv* lost his long ago. He's more wolf than man and more demon than wolf. He was born of the dark, created by the magic Forsaken used to turn him. The dark is all he knows now."

Oh, my God.

"We have to go back," I whisper. "Abigail and the Blooded..." There are countless dozens of people at Eitr, people who will need Dax and his brothers if the *varulv* find the town.

"It's too late to go back. If we try, we lead them right to the gates. All we can do is go forward and pray we stay out of their path," Malachi says. "Hold on to something. It's going to get bumpy."

For the next half hour, we creep through the dark, the forest pressing in on us from all sides. I don't know if the Fae can see anything in the dark, but I can't. Malachi has the headlights off to keep our position hidden. Trees loom up out of nowhere, their branches scraping like fingers along the sides of the truck.

Howls split apart the dark, bouncing back from the mountainside in eerie, distorted echoes that send chills up and down my spine. No one says a word. The walkie-talkie remains silent. Whatever's happening in the valley below happens in silence.

Are the Fae still alive?

Have the *varulv* found Eitr?

The truck crawls to a stop, Malachi muttering a curse. "We're going to have to melt ice if we're going to cross here."

"I'll do it," Reaper says. "Just keep the *jävla helveteshundar* off me if they show up."

I don't know what that means, but judging by how he says it, I can guess. He's talking about the hellhounds, and he wasn't complimenting them.

"*Ja,*" Dax says softly. "We will." He turns to me, cupping my cheek in his palm. "I need you to stay in the truck, *bittesmå ljós*. I must help Reaper."

"Please be careful," I whisper, not asking him to stay. I can't, as much as I want to do exactly that. His brother needs him. Both of them do. I can no more ask him to stay right here in this truck with me as I can ask him to stop being Fae.

"Always." He brushes his lips across mine in a soft pass, and then he and Reaper climb from the truck. The overhead lights momentarily flicker on, allowing me to see what Malachi did.

We're stopped at a rickety wooden bridge that's little more than a few pieces of old wood stretched across the roadway over a creek. The creek is frozen solid, and ice stands several inches thick on the wood. If we tried to drive over it, we'd slide right off the side into the frozen water.

Reaper's *Magn* glows brighter as he calls his *lyststål* to him. A second later, Dax does the same. They jog toward the bridge, their feet soundless over the ice.

"He's one of the strongest warriors we have," Malachi says quietly. "He'll be fine out there."

He will be. He has to be. I refuse to accept anything less. But I still hold my breath anyway, barely daring to breathe as Reaper puts his *lyststål* to the ice, slowly melting through it while Dax guards his back. It takes fifteen minutes to melt enough for Malachi to drive over the bridge.

Once the truck is safely on the other side, Reaper and Dax quickly climb back in.

I burrow into Dax's arms, sending up a prayer of gratitude...though I'm not entirely sure who to address it to any longer. It's been a long, long time since I prayed at all. Now, I'm not sure exactly who listens to our prayers. Not even the Fae know.

"You're freezing," I whisper to Dax, shivering when his cold skin touches mine.

"I am well, *bittesmå ljós*," he promises, pulling me closer. His lips seek mine in the dark, his kiss hot and hungry. A purr rumbles in his chest, sending waves of heat wafting through me. "*Nei*, I am better than well."

"Dax," I hiss.

He laughs, a wicked, devilish sound, and kisses me again.

I groan, burying my face in his throat. He's a wicked, wicked Fae. And I think I love it. No, I know I love it. The last few days have been a whirlwind. But the Fae standing steady at the center of the maelstrom makes my heart race. He's quickly wriggling his way into my heart, taking little pieces I never intended to give him. And I keep willingly handing them over as if it's the most natural thing in the world to do.

"*Faen!*" Malachi hisses, slamming on the brakes.

I lift my head to find out what's happening, just as a chorus of howls rip the night apart, far, far too close. Dax goes rigid, a curse rattling from his lips. Reaper swears, too.

"Drive through them," Dax orders Malachi.

"I can't. There's another bridge ahead."

"*Faen!*"

"They're surrounding the truck."

"Then we stand and fight," Dax says, murderous fury in his voice. Even then, his hands are gentle as he lifts me off him. "As soon as we're out of the truck, climb into the front with Malachi, *lyseste ljós*. I want you glued to his side until I'm back in this truck. Understood?"

"Dax," I whisper, tears welling in my eyes. "Please."

"Understood, Rissa?" he says, shaking me gently.

"Y-yes."

He presses his lips to my forehead. "*Hundre riker ville være for få til å inneholde min kjærlighet til deg.*"

Before I can ask what he said, he pulls free of my arms and flings himself out of the truck, his *lyststål* blazing to life in his hands. Reaper is a step behind him. I clamber over the console, dropping into the seat beside Malachi, trying desperately to keep my gaze on Dax.

I don't see the *varulv* at first. All I see are Dax and Reaper standing back to back, their *lyststål* at the ready. And then a thick shadow moves just beyond them. I rear back in shock, crying out.

The *varulv* are massive black wolves, standing taller than any wolf I've ever seen. Foam flecks their muzzles, their teeth razor-sharp and dripping. Their breath steams before them as they pace closer to Dax and Reaper, staying just out of reach of their *lyststål*.

"Come, *varulv*," Reaper growls. "If you want her so badly, come and get her, you mangy mutts."

"Come taste the wrath of the Fae again," Dax taunts. "Just like you did in Valhalla when we destroyed your kin."

The *varulv* closest to him darts forward, snapping those razor-sharp teeth. Dax spins to the right, his *lyststål* twirling in his hands like a baton. He barely misses the demon wolf. The wolf races out of reach just as the other darts forward, trying to get his teeth around Dax's leg.

Reaper brings his *lyststål* down.

I cry out, startled as the demon's head separates from his body, rolling into the dark.

The other *varulv* howl in fury for their fallen mate. One leaps against the truck, trying to break the glass. I cover my head, certain he's going to smash through the window into the vehicle with us.

Malachi curses up a storm beside me.

A second later, the *varulv* yelps.

"Got the bastard!" Malachi cheers.

I spread my fingers apart to see Dax holding the giant wolf. He tosses him, sending him careening into a tree. Leaves and branches shower down, but it doesn't slow the demon dog any. He's on his feet again in seconds, leaping at Dax's back.

Dax spins with his *lyststål* raised, slicing through the animal's throat. Blood splatters everywhere as the animal falls backward. He doesn't get up again.

Two others flank Reaper, trying to attack from both sides. The beautiful warrior doesn't even look tired as he whirls his *lyststål* overhead, ready to launch it at whichever of the two tries him first. The smile on his face is sinister, deadly. He's enjoying this.

I think they both are.

Dax shakes off the blood of the *varulv* he just killed, stepping up beside Reaper. "Stop playing with your meal, brother. It's not nice."

"Meal?" Reaper scoffs. "These pups aren't even big enough to count as a snack. Letting my *lyststål* taste their blood is almost offensive."

Dax chuckles as the *varulv* closest to him snarls as if he understands the warriors' mocking. "Then let's be done with this and find a more fitting prize to play with."

"*Ja*," Reaper agrees.

They move so quickly I'm not even sure I see them move at all. One minute, they're standing still, talking smack. The next, they're five steps closer to the *varulv*, their *lyststål* whirling so fast they blur. The *varulv* leap at them, snarling and howling. Reaper was right, though. They aren't even a match for the warriors. Within seconds, the demon dogs are dead, their lifeless bodies falling to the ground.

Dax grins at Reaper, releasing his hold on his *lyststål*.

Reaper grins back, nudging one of the *varulv* with his foot. "That almost wasn't worth the effort. Either they've gotten slower over the centuries, or they were new blood."

Dax grunts his agreement. "Let's go melt this ice so we can get out of here before we have to find out one way or another. They weren't the only four in this forest. I hear the others out there still."

"*Ja.*" Reaper jogs toward the bridge ahead, stepping over the bodies of the demon dogs.

"What happens to them?" I ask Malachi. "Will someone stumble across them?"

"Nah," Malachi answers. "Within hours, their bodies will desiccate. After that happens, a stiff enough wind will take care of what's left."

My stomach turns at his explanation, but it settles my mind, too. At least no one will stumble across them and end up hurting themselves, messing with something they don't understand. Humanity is good at that. We're told not to touch, and we can't resist doing exactly that.

I yawn, laying my head against the seatback as I watch Dax and Reaper slowly melting through the ice covering the bridge we need to cross. My eyelids droop, exhaustion trying to drag me under. I float in that void between wakefulness and sleep, my gaze locked on Reaper's *lyststål* as he sweeps it over the ice in careful passes.

A shadow moves in the dark. For a moment, my mind doesn't register it as anything more than the wind rustling through the trees. And then it comes again. I shift my gaze from Reaper, hunting down the shadow.

"Dax!" I scream, flinging myself out of the truck. "*Varulv!*"

Dozens of them slip out of the woods on soundless paws, coming from every direction.

Dax spins toward me, his *lyststål* in his hands. As soon as he sees what I do, horror overtakes his expression. There are too many for them to fight this time. Already, they cut in between the truck and the bridge, cutting off their only route to safety. Cutting us off from one another.

"Get back in the truck!" Dax roars.

"I'm not leaving you!" I cry, tears rolling down my face. What was it he said? A person can't survive with half a soul.

He's right. I can't survive with only half of mine. I don't get a chance to tell him that. I don't get a chance to say anything else.

The *varulv* attack as one mighty force, their howls rending the air.

They advance on Dax and Reaper, snarling and snapping at the air. There are so many of them I lose track of Dax as he rushes into battle, trying to defend himself and his brother.

"Get in the truck, Valkyrie," Malachi says, his *lyststål* blazing as he races around the side of the truck. "Drive through them if you have to do it. Drive through us if you must. But don't get out of the truck no matter what. No matter what happens, the Forsaken cannot take you."

"Malachi," I cry, wrapping my arms around myself.

The giant, friendly Fae roars and plows into the nearest *varulv*, knocking the animal off its feet. They go rolling, knocking several others aside.

I scramble into the truck, sobbing the whole time. My gaze falls on the walkie-talkie. I grab it, hitting the button to talk. "Hello? Hello? Damrion? We need help! We're under attack!"

I release the button, waiting for a response.

None comes.

I try again. "If anyone can hear me, we need help. There are dozens of *varulv*. We can't fight them. We can't..." I sob into the radio. "Please, help us."

Still, no one answers. God, is anyone else even still alive to hear my call? Or are we entirely on our own out here? I don't know. But I can't let Dax die. I can't let his brothers die. This isn't what I was born to do...to die crying in a truck while the man who owns my soul gets torn apart by demon wolves.

For the second time in my life, I intentionally reach for the power Dax is so sure I wield. Not the little bits I've grasped for my entire life. Not strength to get me through a dark moment or courage to face what's in front of me. But the Light of the Valkyrie, the same power my ancestors wielded. They touched souls with that power, united realms, and when they needed to do it, they struck down their enemies with fierce blasts of Light none could withstand. That's what I reach for now.

I fling every door in my soul open to it, allowing it to flood through every cell of my body. I feed my emotions into it—my fear for Dax, my absolute terror that I'm going to fail at this task that's been set before me, the grief I felt standing in the Fae Hall of Warriors, and the fierce, radiant devotion growing in my heart for the Fae whose soul is somehow, in some way, bound to mine. I don't try to keep

Dax out. I don't try to hide from him. In this moment, I'm done hiding from him and fighting what's between us. I let him come flooding in.

Light fills me, too, crackling like electricity. I feel it surging through every fiber of my being, hotter than the sun, more powerful than anything I've ever felt. I climb from the truck, and the world quakes at my feet.

Ice turns to steam beneath my boots. The air steams around me. I march forward, straight toward the *varulv* surrounding the three Fae warriors.

Dax senses me coming. He feels me as if I'm standing beside him, just as I feel him. Pride rolls from him. And fear. Even now, he worries for me. He's afraid for me.

The *varulv* closest to me steps too close to the Light surrounding me and goes up in flames exactly like the Forsaken did at the bar. His screams rend the air, far too human. He falls into another *varulv*, and it ignites too. I keep moving forward, walking right through the center of them. One by one, they ignite. One by one, they die.

Those further out begin to panic. They break ranks, no longer concerned with the warriors or what they came here to do. All they want to do now is survive. They turn to flee into the woods.

I refuse to let them. They aren't of this world, and they aren't of the Light. They were made of darkness to do dark deeds. They cannot be allowed to run free in this world. They're a danger to everyone and everything in it.

I spread my arms wide. Ropes of Light shoot out like bolts of lightning. They spread like spiderwebs across the forest floor. Every *varulv* they touch ignites in a burst of flame, its shadow burning away. I strike again and again, reaching deeper into the forest with every blast of Light.

"Enough, Valkyrie," Dax growls, grasping my shoulders. "Enough!"

"I have to stop them. All of them."

"*Nei.*" He shakes me so hard that he rattles my skull. "Stop before you burn yourself out. Stop!"

The fear in his voice slices through me like a blade, cutting deep. I've never heard his voice tremble like that before. I've never heard it shake. But it shakes now, as if he's terrified.

I release the Light pouring through me all at once...which is apparently the wrong thing to do. It flows back into the well so quickly it's like opening the door on an airplane in midair. Everything gets stuck in a vacuum, the air leaving my lungs in a rush.

I stumble as the world goes dark around the edges, my legs threatening to collapse.

Dax curses, scooping me into his arms before I hit the ground. "Rissa, Valkyrie," he whispers, pressing his face to my throat. "*Lyseste ljós. Du er i min verden.*"

"You're going to have to teach me your language, Dax. I don't understand you," I mumble, my eyes falling closed.

I don't hear his response. For a long time, I don't hear anything at all.

Chapter Nine

Dax

"How is she?" Damrion asks.

"Sleeping." I don't take my gaze from my Valkyrie as my oldest friend enters the nondescript room, pulling the door closed behind him. Unlike Eitr, our safehouse in the city isn't a place of beauty. It's a converted warehouse overlooking the Sound. The back butts up against a sheer cliff, making an attack from behind impossible. A massive chain-link fence surrounds the rest. No one knows that the pallets of wood scattered around the lower floor are just a front to hide the true purpose of this place. "Malachi told you what happened?"

"Reaper did." Damrion watches her intently. "You should know...she didn't just kill the *varulv* in the forest. She killed those in the valley, too."

"Gods have mercy," I whisper, stunned. I knew she was powerful, but what we're talking about? Not even the Gods wielded that sort of power. She killed hundreds tonight, every *varulv* her Light touched. It'll take centuries before the Forsaken are able to replenish their numbers. Centuries before the hellhounds are half the threat they've been for millennia.

"We lost a warrior tonight."

"Who?"

"Arundiel."

"*Faen*." I scowl at the concrete floor of the safe house. Arundiel was one of our oldest warriors. He was a formidable Fae.

"They sent twelve Forsaken to capture her."

"Twelve Forsaken for a single Valkyrie," I whisper, shaking my head as my gaze drifts back to the woman sleeping in the bed beside me. She's so peaceful and still. At rest, she looks as young and innocent as ever. Her Light is little more than a golden glow around her, a tiny fraction of the true power she wields. I know the true scope of it, though. Even now, I feel it inside her, blazing like one thousand suns. "They have to know what she's capable of."

"*Ja*," Damrion says. "They do."

"Abigail?" I ask, the one topic we've avoided since Rissa raised the possibility that the Forsaken were sending the girl's visions. It's a troubling possibility, the implications grim. But if there's even a slim chance that Rissa is right and the Forsaken have worked out how to send visions to Abigail, we have to consider that they've also figured out how to siphon off images from her true visions. If they're using her as a bridge to the Fae, as a conduit into our council, Gods only knows what they've seen. Clearly enough to send nearly every *varulv* they have into the mountains. Enough to send twelve Forsaken after Rissa.

"Possibly," Damrion says, his lips twisted as if the word tastes bitter upon them. "*Faen*. I don't want to believe it. She's a shining Light."

"*Ja*, she is. One no one would ever suspect. It makes her the perfect candidate, Damrion. That doesn't make her guilty of anything more than that. She hasn't sold her soul to the dark. They use her without her consent or knowledge. If Rissa is right, it means only that we must be careful going forward. We cannot blindly trust her visions to guide us any longer."

Damrion jerks his head in a nod. "Which means we have no idea why we're really here," he says.

I cock my head to the side, not sure what he's getting at.

"We don't know if they sent the vision that led us here or if it's a true vision," he says. "My gut tells me it's a trap they've set for the Valkyrie. One she's willing to walk into to free the people she loves. But if it's a true vision, she was always meant to come back to Seattle. So why try to trap her in the valley tonight at all?"

It's an excellent question. One I hadn't considered until just now. I was operating under the assumption that the Forsaken and *varulv* attacked to get to her, but if she was destined to return to Seattle, they had to know that wouldn't work. They had to know they were wasting their numbers in a doomed attempt. As far as we know, not even the Forsaken can circumvent Abigail's visions. What she sees always comes to pass. Always.

"Abigail," I say. "They want Abigail." Whatever they're planning, they don't want to risk us seeing it.

"*Ja*," Damrion growls, his expression fierce. "I believe so."

"Have you warned the warriors in Eitr?"

"I have. Two dozen guard her and Letty as we speak. They'll continue in shifts until we're back in Eitr." He blows out a sharp breath. "I'd bring her here if I thought it was any safer."

"Eitr is the safest place for her. It's always been the safest place for her." As the Forsaken learned tonight, getting to her won't be a walk in the park for them. Even without Rissa's power, getting up the mountain is no easy feat. Neither is locating Eitr. If they're lucky enough to do it, they still have to battle their way through scores of Fae warriors—every single one willing to die where he stands to protect every one of the Blooded in town.

"*Ja*, I know." Damrion scrubs a hand down his face. "It does not make me worry any less, brother. As Rissa reminded us today, Abigail may be powerful, but she's still human. And when I agreed to allow her to stay, I made a vow to ensure she was well cared for and happy."

"You've kept your vow, brother."

He nods, though he doesn't look any less troubled. Damrion always worries too much. He carries the weight of the world on his shoulders and always has. That's the price of leadership. He never complains. He simply shoulders the burden and continues on. But it isn't easy. I suspect, sometimes, it's the hardest thing in the world.

"Adriel does not agree," he says after a moment. "He's furious that we left her behind."

"*Nei*," I say quietly. "Adriel is furious that the only person he's opened his heart to in two thousand years is in danger, and he's helpless to do anything about it." He's a complicated Fae, but this, I understand completely. Adriel would move heaven and earth to protect Abigail, just like

Damrion would. And right now, there's nothing either of them can do for her. Damrion blames himself. Adriel blames himself. But he lashes out at Damrion, just like he's always done.

Even now, Adriel loves Damrion. He's just too angry to admit it. He was abandoned when he needed him most. In two thousand years, the sting of that still hasn't faded. It might not ever. But sooner or later, one of them will be forced to admit what they both fight so hard to deny. They aren't brothers. They never have been. This is more than that. That's why it cuts them both so damn deeply. Perhaps Abigail is a part of that. Perhaps she isn't. I don't know. I don't pretend to see the patterns in the tapestry the Norns weave.

But the three of them can only circle one another for so long before the Norns either push them together or pull them apart. One day soon, one or the other will happen. It's only a matter of time.

Half an hour after Damrion slips from the room in the old Fae safehouse, Rissa begins to stir. I'm back at her side in an instant, kneeling beside the bed with my hands on her cheeks.

"Valkyrie," I breathe as her eyes flutter and slowly open. "You're back with me."

Confusion cuts through her gaze before those bright blue pools land on me. As soon as they do, relief washes over her. I see it take her, relaxing her muscles and the furrow between her brows.

"Dax," she whispers. "I had the worst dream."

I don't have the heart to tell her it was no dream.

"All is well, *lyseste ljós*. You're safe."

Apparently, though I say little, I still manage to speak too much.

Her expression falls.

"It wasn't a dream."

I don't lie to her. I cannot.

"*Nei*, Valkyrie. It was no dream."

"Did I..." She pauses to wet her bottom lip with the tip of her tongue. "Did I kill them?"

"You can't kill what's already dead, Rissa."

"You keep saying that," she whispers.

"Because it's true." I stroke my fingertips along her cheeks. "I won't allow you to carry guilt that doesn't belong to you. The *varulv* willingly sold their souls to the dark upon death. They allowed the Forsaken to twist what they were into what they became. They were already dead. There was no Light in them left to extinguish, just like there is none left in the Forsaken. You expose the shadow in their twisted souls to the Light, a Light they haven't felt fall upon them in Gods only know how long. That isn't death. That's mercy."

"They screamed like they were dying," she mutters, shivering at the memory.

"Dark doesn't give way to Light easily, *lyseste ljós*."

She frowns at me.

"When you turn on the light in a room, does the shadow hide, or does the light vanquish it?" I ask her.

"How should I know?"

"Humor me, Rissa."

"I don't know, Dax. I never thought about it. I just turn on the light."

"*Ja*. You just turn on the light, and the shadow goes away. The same thing happens here. You shine your Light, and the shadow burns away. But if the shadows in that room could speak, do you think they'd go silently, *lyseste ljós*? Or do you think they'd scream their defiance the whole way?"

"I don't know. I never thought about it," she whispers. "I guess they'd probably scream."

"*Ja*. They would. The dark doesn't give way to the Light easily," I repeat. "It goes with a scream of fury, reminded that the only thing more powerful than the dark is the Light. The only thing capable of defeating the dark and burning away those shadows is the one thing it loathes. *Light*." I brush my thumbs across her cheeks. "They didn't scream as if they were dying, Rissa. They screamed in horror. They screamed in rage. For the first time in thousands of years, the Light fell upon them, and they were forced to remember what they willingly gave up."

"Their humanity?"

"Love. *Alt du gjør er gjort i kjærlighet.*"

Her gaze flits across my face, searching. "Sometimes, I feel like what you say is right at the forefront of my mind, as if I should be able to remember it, and I just can't recall. It's so familiar, even though I've never heard the language before."

"Your heart remembers, Valkyrie, even if your mind does not."

"What did you say?"

"I said that all you do, you do in love."

"Oh." She swallows audibly, her throat working. "You felt what I did tonight, didn't you?"

"*Ja*," I whisper.

"I couldn't let you die trying to protect me, Dax. You said a person can't live with only half a soul. You were right. I can't live with only half of mine," she whispers, tears shimmering in her lashes. "If you die...I can't...I don't..." She licks her lips and tries again. "I don't want to live in this world without you."

"What are you saying, Valkyrie?"

"I'm saying..." She blows out a breath. "Whatever I have to do to complete this bond, I'll do. Whatever it takes to bind my soul to yours, I'm in. I want it, Dax."

This is the place humans call heaven. This is rapture. It must be because I've traveled the realms with the Valkyrie. I've walked the Shining City and knelt in the Hall of Warriors. I've raced through the forests of *Álfheimr* and bathed in its deepest pools. Every haven of Light, I've seen. But none come close to this drafty room and this one perfect, peaceful moment. None could even hope to compare to the Valkyrie spread across the bed, her bright blue eyes locked on my face. This has to be rapture, because I know no other name for the soul-deep sense of wonder coursing through me. There is no word for the adoration pumping through my veins.

Ja. All we do, we do for love. I'd raze kingdoms and destroy realms in the name of it. Just for one more moment with this powerful Valkyrie. That's how completely she owns my soul. That's how wildly my Fae heart beats for her.

"Rissa," I breathe, crawling onto the bed with her, pride and awe and joy crashing together in the center of my chest. "My Valkyrie."

"Tell me what to do, Dax," she whispers, draping her arms around my neck. "Tell me how to complete it."

"You already have, Valkyrie," I breathe, leaning down to press my lips to hers in a fervent, devoted kiss. My tongue tangles with hers, drawing her taste into my mouth, her breath into my lungs. "When you thought I was in danger, you threw your soul open wide to me. You allowed me to claim it."

Even in the middle of battle, I didn't hesitate. Some things are more important than death and killing. Some things matter more than the war between Light and Dark. Binding this Valkyrie to me, claiming my place in her soul, is one of those things. It's the *only* thing.

She arches beneath me, mewling sweetly. Her hands slip through my hair, clutching at the strands, the move almost raw and desperate, as if the unrelenting desire of the bond has finally caught up with her, demanding an outlet. As if she needs me as desperately as I need her.

Her Light calls me, beckoning me closer, compelling me to her. Does she even know she does it? Shines her

Light upon me every time I touch her? Does she feel her soul responding to mine every time my mouth moves with hers? Gods help me, does she have any concept of what it does to me to feel her, not Fae to Valkyrie, but man to woman?

I ache for her in ways I cannot put to words. There are none for the hunger she sends raging through me with every beat of my heart.

I flip her over, praying the change of position grants me a modicum of control. It does not.

She settles over me, her hips flush with mine. The heat of her center nestles against my cock. My teeth ache from her sweetness.

"Rissa," I groan, breaking our kiss. "You kiss me, and I forget the dark exists."

"Then let's deny its existence a little while longer, Dax," she demands. "Kiss me again."

"Valkyrie."

She growls as if she thinks I intend to deny her—as if I could—and leans down, biting my bottom lip. I growl, arching my hips into hers as the small pain mixes with pleasure, making my cock throb for her.

"Do not play with fire you do not understand, *bittesmå ljós*," I warn, gripping onto her hips.

"Didn't you know, Adaxiel?" She smiles at me, a womanly, triumphant smile full of raw, feminine energy. "I was born of the Light. I was made to burn."

I growl, leaning up to press my mouth to hers again. I slip my hands beneath her shirt, dragging it up her body. Her skin is soft and warm beneath my hands, like the smoothest silk. The rush of sensation spiraling through me is indescribable, like hurting through the skies, sheltered in the rays of the sun.

I break away from her lips to pull her shirt over her head. It falls beside the bed. When I try to kiss her again, she leans out of my reach. I watch through slit lids, annoyed that she doesn't obey when I want her lips on mine. Turned on that she doesn't give me what I want when I want it. She taunts and teases, forcing me to patience when I have none.

Her center grinds against me as she shifts around, her eyes wide and her lips swollen from my kisses. So radiantly beautiful.

She grows even more radiant when she reaches behind her, deftly unhooking her bra. It falls forward, held to her body by the thin straps across her pale shoulders. Those, she slides slowly from her body, her eyes locked with mine as if daring me to stop her.

As if I can. As if I would.

Her bra falls between us, leaving her nude from the waist up.

"Sweet, merciful Light," I breathe, staring in a daze. I ache to touch her, to feel her alabaster skin beneath my palms and lips again. But I've never felt more unworthy. She is perfection, starlight and sunlight poured into mortal form.

There's a reason she was born only now, so long after the Gods walked the earth. Had they looked upon her, they would have trembled in rage at her beauty, so much more radiant than theirs. And at her power, so much purer than theirs. She was not made of Light, she *is* Light. And Gods save me, but I intend to capture it for myself.

I swallow against the need burning through me, against the depths of my desire. Gods, I've never felt anything like it. But it isn't only mine I feel. *Nei*. It's hers, reflected back to me like thousands of stars scattered through the night sky.

This is what it is to love a Valkyrie.

This is what it is to be loved by a Valkyrie.

A low groan tumbles from my lips, gratitude and desire crashing together as she throws open the doors of her soul and allows me to step through again, opening herself to me in every way.

I tumble her over backward, falling upon her like a Fae possessed. She cries out, clutching me to her as I run my hands up and down her sides, latching onto one hardened peak.

"Dax!" She bows off the bed, my name echoing around us.

"*Ja*," I breathe against her skin. "Dax. Your mate. Keeper of your soul." I nip her skin again and then again, helpless to stop myself as she writhes in pleasurable torment every time my teeth touch her skin. I feel her pleasure as acutely as I do my own.

I prowl down her body, reveling in the way she responds to me. Marveling in the way she's right there, nestled inside my head as if she's always been there. As if that little corner was always reserved for her. Pleasure after pleasure whispers from it, flowing through me like ropes of gold.

I kiss across her round belly, nuzzling the softness there. I nip and bite, dragging my teeth down her lower abdomen.

She cries out for me, singing sweetly.

I drag her pants down her legs, desperate to taste her as no one else has. As no one ever will. Every part of her will be mine, just as every part of me will belong to her and her alone. That is the future the Norns wove for us. That's the fate I fight for now. If Valhalla must fall forever to save this Valkyrie, so be it.

"Ah, Rissa," I groan, my gaze falling on her wet sex. She's beautiful here too. As pink as the heart-shaped flowers that grew wild on the hillside in *Álfheimr*. She's dripping wet, her hard little clit swollen and aching for attention.

"Dax, please," she pleads. "Please, it hurts."

"Not for long, *bittesmå ljós*." I shoulder my way between her legs, lifting her to my lips. My tongue slides through her folds.

Her keening cry rips through the room, setting me ablaze with her Light. I growl in response—a wordless battle cry, a prayer of devotion—and drag her closer. What control I had, she wrests from me with that single sound, with the weight of her emotions. With the feel of her nestled in my soul, sharing her pleasure and unfettered joy with me.

I eat her as a starving man eats, rudely, slovenly. I am greedy with her, taking, taking, taking. She gives of herself freely, sobbing my name into the room for all to hear. I don't care if every Fae in the safehouse hears her cries and knows that the bond is complete. In this moment, I don't care if every Forsaken in the city senses her and knows we're here.

Let them come. Let them try to wrest this Valkyrie from my arms. They'll fall where they stand.

I lave the flat of my tongue against her clit, driving her higher, and then higher still. She mewls and cries and shouts, giving herself over entirely to the pleasure. She doesn't fight it. She doesn't fight me. She falls into it, falls into *us*.

And when she shatters, she does so with a piercing cry of joy that sends shockwaves rocketing through me. I eat her through it, not letting up until she falls limp into my hands.

I lay her gently against the bed, rising to strip from my clothes. She watches through slit lids, trembling as her gaze drifts all over me, eating me alive. The minute I drag my pants down, her eyes fly open wide.

"Dax," she whispers, strangled.

"All is well, *bittesmå ljós*," I promise, crawling onto the bed with her. I am not a small Fae, and human males are not equipped the same. Perhaps I should have warned her, but I did not think about it.

"What..." She licks her lips, staring up at me. "Is that a...barb?"

"*Nei*. We call it a knot."

"What is it?"

"Come here." I roll onto my back beside her, reaching for her hand so she can see for herself. She scrambles to her knees, kneeling beside me. Strands of her long hair sweep across my chest, causing my cock to stiffen further.

She stares in fascination. She doesn't seem repulsed or afraid. If anything, she seems...turned on by the thought of the knot. *Interesting.*

"Touch me, Valkyria. Feel for yourself."

She lifts one hand as if in a daze, slowly reaching for me. Her hand glides down my abdomen, her fingertips barely kissing the head of my cock. I growl, my hips lifting from the bed.

"Someone is impatient," she teases.

"*Ja*, this Fae," I growl.

Her soft laughter washes over me.

She runs the back of her hand down my shaft, still teasing. I grit my teeth, determined to let her have her way. Even if it kills me. My body is hers to command.

"You're so hard," she whispers. "Does it hurt?"

"Like your hell."

She finally takes pity on me, wrapping her hand around my shaft. My hips lift from the bed again, a groan rolling from my hips. Gods alive. Her Light sears everywhere her skin touches mine, sinking deep.

"Valkyrie," I choke. "Gods have mercy."

She runs her wicked, brilliant hand up and down, stroking as if she knows exactly what she's doing to me. I think, perhaps, she does. She can feel me as well as I do her. The minute she opened her soul to me willingly last night—not in a moment of panic or fear but because she wanted the bond between us—she forged that link. We can mute it. We can mask it if we must. But it will never, ever fade.

"Tell me what it is, Adaxiel," she commands. "I want to know."

"The knot was designed for breeding, Rissa," I rasp, trying to focus as she torments me. "When a Fae finds his mate, the knot helps ensure his seed stays right where it's meant to be. So long as the knot is inside you, I cannot leave your perfect body."

Her hand falters on me. For a moment, my heart sinks. I convince myself she isn't ready. Of course she isn't. Just a few short days ago, this world didn't even exist to her. And now I'm asking her not just for her heart and soul, but for her womb, too?

For a moment, I know shame. It cuts me to the bone.

And then her grip tightens on me, and my gaze flies to hers.

"I want it inside me, Dax," she whispers, her eyes glowing. She clambers over me, straddling my thighs. "*Now.*"

Who am I to deny a Valkyrie, the most worthy among us?

I grip her hips, dragging her higher. The heat of her center kisses the head of my cock, and we both throw our heads back, crying out into the room. Gods alive. I might not survive the heat of her wrapped around me. But if I die, at least I'll have known what it means to be complete at least once in this life. At least I'll die in her arms.

A Fae can only hope to have such an easy death. Most Fae warriors die bloody. That's the fate woven into the tapestry for most of us. We accepted it long ago. But even those of us sworn to guard Valhalla still dream.

"Gods, *bittesmå ljós*," I growl, writhing as she grinds against me, slowly driving me mad. I halt her with my hands on her hips, lifting up to claim her lips in a wild kiss. "No more before you ruin me."

"That's the plan, Dax." She nips my bottom lip. "To ruin you."

I growl a warning, lifting her slightly to notch my cock at her entrance. "Perhaps I'll ruin you first, little Valkyrie."

"Do it," she breathes, as fearless now as ever. "Ruin us, Adaxiel."

"Come to me, *elskan-ljós*," I purr, sitting up slightly. I slip my hand into her hair. "Come to me."

She presses her lips to mine, accepting my kiss willingly. I drag her down on me, writhing in the sweetest torment as her body stretches to accommodate me. Gods have mercy...

"Rissa," I groan, unsure where my pleasure ends and hers begins. If there's pain for her, I can't find it in the sea of sensation ripping through us. I don't think she can, either. She shakes on top of me, her mouth open wide, her eyes glossy.

"Dax. Oh, God, Dax." Her nails dig into my shoulders, shredding my skin as she drags herself down on top of me, eagerly taking more. It's as if she can't stop herself now that she's started.

I grip her hips, trying to slow her down when I feel her barrier, but she clenches her inner muscles as if she knows what I'm doing. My control slips. I jerk my hips without intending to do so.

We both gasp as her barrier gives way.

"You did that on purpose," I growl, biting her bottom lip.

"*Ja*," she whispers, writhing on top of me. "I'm not delicate, Dax. Don't treat me like I am."

Nei, she isn't delicate. She's fiercer than any warrior I've ever met. I've known fully trained warriors who would have broken in the face of such overwhelming odds last night. Not Rissa. She didn't waver.

"Are you all right, *elskan-ljós*?"

"Perfect," she promises. "So perfect, Dax."

"Then move with me, little warrior." I lift her an inch and drop her, showing her how to fuck. She moans, those little claws digging into my shoulders again. I lick and kiss her neck as she rocks her hips, searching for a rhythm more instinctive than breathing.

It takes only moments for her to find it. She uses her grip on my shoulders to balance herself as she lifts herself up and drops back down on me. Pleasure blasts down the bridge connecting us every time her bottom lands against my thighs. Hers. Mine. I hardly know.

I flip her backward, following her over. Desperate to be the one who drives her crazy now. She mewls as I drag her leg up over my hip, opening her to me. I attack her breasts with lips and teeth and tongue, using everything at my disposal to make this little Valkyrie sing as I pound into her, fucking her over and over.

She comes apart around me, crying out my name. I growl and go harder, deeper, no longer afraid of hurting her or taking too much. I cannot. She was made for me, the same I was made for her. I pour myself into her, fucking into her again and then again.

Her voice breaks as I flip her onto her stomach, taking her from behind. It's deeper this way. She's more obedient this way. I stare at the way I disappear into her, spellbound.

"I look good covered in you, Valkyrie," I tell her, sinking my hand into her hair to crane her head back. My lips come down on hers in a punishing kiss. "You look good taking me."

"Dax," she whimpers.

"This is what it is to be loved by a Fae." We aren't gentle creatures. But neither are Valkyrie. And she gives as well as she takes, scratching and clawing. Biting. Her claw marks adorn my back and shoulders. Her bite marks litter my chest.

I flip her again, needing her eyes on me when I knot her. If for no other reason than because I want her to know that she's mine in that way. That it's my seed deep in her belly, and my knot keeping it there.

"You want to come again, *lyseste ljós*?" I ask, reaching between us to stroke her clit.

She shakes her head, gasping. "I can't. I can't."

"*Ja*, you can. You will."

"Dax."

"Outside of this bed, your word is law, Valkyrie," I murmur, brushing tangles of hair from her face. "I'll obey every command you give, even to the death. But in this bed, I make the rules. And *you* obey." I nuzzle her throat, pressing my lips against her ear as I stroke her clit, pumping into her at the same time. "That's what it is to love this Fae, Rissa."

"Dax," she groans, her inner muscles clenching and fluttering around me. Her Light crackling like electricity gathering in the sky. She blazes brighter and brighter still, on the edge of an orgasm bigger than anything she's ever known. I feel it building in her, threatening to annihilate her entire world.

"*Jeg elsker deg*," I breathe against her skin, hoping to send her over the edge. "I love you."

She flares brighter than a supernova, splintering apart in a shower of Light that turns the room around us white. Not a single sound passes her lips, yet I hear the truth whispering from her soul as if she screamed it into a megaphone.

I love you, Dax.

I roar in triumph, in surrender, and release my power over her as my knot catches, tying us together. Her body goes rigid beneath me, another orgasm crashing into her as everything in my soul hits her in a tidal wave and she feels the knot for the first time.

I bury my face in her throat, groaning as my seed pours into her in a hot flood. She writhes and moans, nails scrabbing down my back.

"Dax, Dax," she cries. "I feel it. Oh, God, I feel it."

I growl, turning my face to claim her mouth as another wave of lust roars through me at her words, threatening to send us both up in flame all over again. Gods alive. If this is what the bond is like with a Valkyrie, I understand completely why no warrior ever survived the loss of it.

How could they? Why would they even want to try?

Chapter Ten

Rissa

"Stop looking at me like that," I whisper, covering my face as Dax stares at me, smirking as if he knows a secret. He's been looking at me the same way for hours. I've never seen him smile so much. I've never seen him so happy.

It looks good on him.

"*Nei*, Valkyrie. I won't," he says, gently prying my hands away from my face. "I'm not ashamed of what they heard. Nor should you be."

"They heard everything, Dax," I hiss. "*Everything*."

"Not everything," he says, still smirking.

I smack him with a pillow, earning a laugh from him.

"All is well, Rissa," he murmurs, drawing me into his arms. "They will not treat you any differently. If anything, you've become something even more precious to all of us now. It's been a long time since a Fae took a mate."

"Really?" I arch my brows, surprised. "None of the Fae ever wed?"

"Not the Fae in Valhalla. We could no more split our focus between a mate and our oath as we could between a single Valkyrie and our oath," he says, taking a big bite of the sandwich Damrion brought a little while ago. He chews and swallows before saying anything else. "No Fae has taken a mate since *Álfheimr* fell."

"Not even here on earth?"

"*Nei*," he says, nudging my plate toward me. "You should eat, *bittesmå ljós*."

I obediently take another bite of my sandwich, though I'm not very hungry. Honestly, I'm more worried than anything. Now that we're here, I'm not quite sure what to do. Since I'm technically missing, I can't go anywhere. Otherwise, I'm going to have to answer a whole bunch of questions I don't know how to answer. Like where I've been for the last few days and why I didn't let anyone know I was leaving. There are limits to what the Fae can accomplish with their compulsion gift. Staying out of sight, especially with the Forsaken on the loose, is our best bet.

So I made a list earlier of everyone I know in Seattle for the Fae to check on them.

Well, almost everyone. There was one name I couldn't add to that list. One name I can't let Dax know about. If the Forsaken are watching my father, Dax will walk right into their trap to kill him. And if they've already taken him...well, I'm not sure I want to know what Dax will do. Let them kill him? Mount a rescue mission so he can kill the man himself?

Either is a possibility.

I hate keeping this from him, but I can't risk his Light. The Fae need it too badly. We need it too badly. I feel helpless, as useless here as I was in Eitr. Part of me wishes the Forsaken would attack already, though I have no idea what I'm supposed to do if and when they do.

Sure, I may be able to burn out their shadows, but the part of that lesson Dax forgot was the part about there always being another shadow waiting in the wings. As soon as the Light goes out, another shadow sweeps in. They wait just out of reach, looking for any opening.

The Forsaken have had two thousand years to grow their ranks mostly unchecked. For the last three hundred years, they've been entirely unchecked. I'm one Valkyrie, standing against an army. If others are supposed to join the fight, we need to find them.

Until then, for all my power, I might as well be a fly buzzing around a giant.

"Your thoughts are dark," Dax murmurs, setting his plate aside. "What are they?"

Crap. I may never get used to the fact that he can read me like a book now. As soon as I start thinking things I shouldn't, he's there, worrying about me, fretting over me. It's sweet to know this Fae warrior cares so much about what's in my mind. No one has cared for me like that since my mom.

"I was thinking about the Forsaken," I admit. "And about the other Valkyrie. And about everything, really. Abigail's vision says I needed to come here, so we're here. But now, I don't know what to do. What happens next? Maybe I should just walk out into the proverbial street and ring the dinner bell for the Forsaken."

"*Nei*," Dax growls, his expression dark. "We will not dangle you like bait, Rissa."

"Then what do we do, Dax?"

"We wait."

"For what?" I cry, frustrated. "For them to start killing people? For them to kill more of your people? How is that an answer?"

He sighs, seeming weary in a way he never has before. Has he slept more than an hour or two at a time since he found me at the bar? I don't think so. He snatches sleep from the jaws of a shark, scooping it out by the thimble full.

"Damrion suspects the point of getting you here was to divide us," he says. "He believes their true target may be Abigail."

My heart sinks. "Eitr is at risk?"

"Eitr has been at risk since the moment the portal dropped us there, *bittesmå ljós*. The life of a Fae is a life of risk. If the Forsaken want Abigail now, the warriors we brought here won't be enough to stop them."

"No, but I might," I whisper.

"I considered that," he admits.

"Why didn't you tell me?"

"Because Abigail is surrounded by the might of the Fae. The people you love are not. They're in just as much danger as she is," he says. "More, perhaps. You made the only choice you could make. Even had you known, this was still the right choice."

"I still should have been told," I growl, glaring at him. "It's not fair for you to keep things from me, Dax. Especially something like this."

"Your duty is to the realms, Rissa," he says. "Mine is now to you and you alone. I won't beg an apology for protecting you from the things that hurt you."

"Don't you get it, Dax? You can't protect me from this!" I cry, scrambling to my feet. "There is an endless well of pain and grief and hard decisions coming our way. You can't protect me from those. I have to know what's happening. It's the only way I can do what I have to do."

"The only thing you have to do is survive, Rissa." He rises to his feet like a lion, lethal and elegant. "That's the only task before you right now. Your survival."

"We both know that's not true."

"For this moment, it is. What comes will come. But for this moment, for today, all you have to do is survive. That's how you serve the realms. You survive. You find a way to keep surviving. And you let me do what I'm sworn to do and protect you from the things that threaten you and your heart. There will be time for you to fight later. The realms will need that warrior's spirit and your power later. But right now, we need you alive." He stops in front of me, crooking a finger beneath my chin. "You can't save everyone. You can't fight every battle. I didn't tell you what would have only hurt you."

"I'm afraid for her," I whisper. I don't care about the implications of the Forsaken getting their hands on her. I'm sure Dax and his brothers have already considered those. I'm afraid *for her*. She's only eighteen, her life barely even started. She's been so brave and fought so hard already. If the Forsaken take her... I don't even want to consider what they'll do to her. Her Light is so bright.

"*Ja*, I know," Dax says, pulling me into his arms. "But the warriors won't let her fall. If it's Abigail they're after, the Fae won't let them take her."

I send up a silent prayer, asking whatever God is in charge to make it so.

"All will be well, Rissa," Dax vows.

"Then make me forget," I plead, throwing myself at him, desperate to think about anything other than the fact that my friends are in danger and there's not a damn thing I can do about it. "Please, Dax, make me forget."

"*Ja*," he whispers, sweeping me up in his arms to carry me toward the bed. "*Ja*."

The next two days pass in a blur. The only way I know that time passes at all is the clock over Dax's bed, and the warriors who come and go. Every day, they leave to check on the people on my list. I pace endlessly while they're gone, waiting for them to return with news.

Dax tries to distract me. He tries to keep my mind occupied. We make love and talk endlessly. But during those hours, there is no distracting me. There is no occupying my mind. All I can do is pace and pray.

On the third day, Stephan and Garrison bring me an *ímun-laukr*, a sword. It's not nearly as large or long as what they carry. In truth, it's more dagger than sword. But the two human warriors spend half the day teaching me to use it while Dax watches carefully. He won't allow them to touch me. As soon as they get too close, he turns into a snarling beast.

But between the three of them, they work out a system for teaching me the basics. Stephan and Garrison show me what to do, and Dax helps ensure I'm holding the weapon correctly. I practice on him.

I expect to hate every minute of it, but I find that I don't hate it at all. With the weapon in my hand, I don't feel useless or helpless. It feels familiar, as if I've worked through the forms a thousand times before. But the knowledge is muted and far away, as if it comes from a dream.

Perhaps it does. I've certainly dreamed of wars and fighting for long enough.

"You did well," Stephan says, grinning at me at the end of the day. "A few more years like today, and you'll be as fierce on a battlefield as your mate."

"A few years?" Garrison snorts. "Give her a few months, and she'll be able to carve your fucking heart out with the thing with both eyes closed." He eyes me with a new respect. I think that's rare for him. He seems like it takes a lot to earn his respect. "You did well."

"Thanks," I whisper, holding the weapon out for him.

"Keep it," he says. "Consider it a gift."

I glance to Dax, who shrugs as if to say this is between me and the two Blooded warriors. "Thank you," I say. "I'll take good care of it."

The warrior nods and then he and Stephan let themselves out of the room. I turn to Dax, surprised. "Did you ask them to come?"

"Nei," he says. "I suspect they made the decision themselves. They're restless without anyone to train."

"They train the warriors?"

"They train with the warriors," he says. "And they train the Blooded who want to learn to fight."

I place the *ímun-laukr* on the small table. "How many Blooded live in Eitr, Dax?"

"At last count? Four hundred and nine."

I spin to face him, shocked. "There are over four hundred of the Blooded there?"

He nods. "There are many, many more than that on Earth, Valkyrie. Thousands, now. But very few are able to touch the Light. Those who can have been showing up at the gates for the last few years, first in a trickle and then in a flood."

"They just show up?"

"*Ja*. They feel what's coming like a shift in the air. I don't know if they even know what they're looking for when they set out, but they seem to find their way to us regardless."

"And they just accept all of this?" I ask. "Just like that?"

"*Nei*, not just like that," he says with a chuckle. "It's no easier for them than it was for you, Rissa. But did you never feel different growing up, as if you didn't quite belong?"

"I did," I whisper. "All the time. I thought something was wrong with me."

"They felt the same."

I'm still processing this when Damrion pounds on the door. "Dax! I need to talk to you in private."

Dax groans, casting his eyes up at the ceiling. "If he and Adriel don't figure it out soon," he mutters before shifting his gaze to me. "Will you be okay by yourself, Valkyrie?"

"I'll be fine, Dax." I roll my eyes. "You worry too much."

"*Ja*." He reaches out, pulling me into his arms to kiss me. "It's my greatest pleasure."

"I love you," I whisper.

"More than the realms themselves," he says, releasing me.

I smile as he slips out into the hall to talk to Damrion. I'm halfway to the shower when he masks the bond between us for the first time ever. One moment, I feel him as if he's still standing next to me. The next, it's as if he's a thousand miles away. The juxtaposition is jarring.

My hackles rise, suspicion immediately flaring to life inside me. I drop the small pile of clothes on the bed, circling back to the bedroom door. I press my ear against the metal, listening intently.

If he and Damrion are still in the hall, they're speaking too quietly to hear.

I risk cracking the door open an inch to check. The hallway is clear.

Where did they go? More importantly, what are they talking about that Dax doesn't want me to know anything about?

I slip into the hallway, pulling the door closed behind me. My feet are soundless on the concrete as I creep down the hall, my back against the wall to avoid detection. I stop at each room along the way, pressing my ear to the door to listen.

"Her father isn't in prison."

I draw up short as Damrion's voice floats up to me from below. My heart lodges itself in my throat, beads of sweat breaking out all over my body.

No. Oh, no.

"What?"

"Malachi ran the name through the system like you asked. He thought it was a pointless request since there's no way for the Forsaken to slip someone out of a prison undetected, but he ran it anyway," Damrion says, his voice soft. "Her father was released two years ago, Dax."

"*Faen*," Dax growls. "She must not know."

I'm sorry. I'm so sorry.

"She testified at his parole hearing," Damrion says. "She knows."

"She lied to me." I hear the sorrow in Dax's voice. Even with the bond masked, I feel little pinpricks of it floating through. They're echoes of echoes, but even those bring tears to my eyes.

I did lie to him, and I'm a hypocrite for doing it. But I'd do the same thing if I had it to do again. His soul is worth saving, even if I have to save it from him. I can't allow him to get his hands on my father. Maybe my father does deserve to die for what he did to me and my mom. But if there's Light left in the realms, it's because we don't decide that. We aren't judge, jury, and executioner, meant to cut down the guilty for their crimes. We hold to the Light, even when it's hard. Even when the dark tempts us.

It's the only way we preserve the Light. It's the only way we *deserve* to preserve it.

"Malachi sent us out looking for the man," Damrion says. "He hasn't been to work in days."

"Forsaken?"

"*Ja*," Damrion says. "Dozens of them. They're crawling all over his place." He hesitates. "And her father isn't the only one they're holding, either. As of a few hours ago, two of her coworkers have gone missing. Genevieve and Jessa. They never returned from lunch."

No. Oh, God, no.

I clamp my hand over my mouth, trying to stifle a sob. Genevieve and Jessa were the only real friends I ever made. They were the only people who never treated me like I was different, or like I was a freak, or like there was something wrong with me. They treated me like I was completely normal.

They're completely normal. They won't understand any of this. How could they? Their lives revolve around boys and makeup and our crappy call-center job. Prophecies and the Forsaken and the battle between Light and Dark are so far beyond anything they know.

I knew it was coming, but I still didn't expect it to hurt this bad. I still didn't expect the guilt to be this overwhelming. They've done nothing wrong...nothing except befriend me. And now, their lives and their souls are in danger. All because they were nice to me.

Dax was right. The Forsaken are soul-damned. Because only monsters prey on those incapable of defending themselves.

"Damrion!" Reaper roars from somewhere down below. "Eitr is under attack. The Forsaken are at the gates."

Chapter Eleven

Dax

R*ISSA LIED TO ME.* Fury twists through me, rattling my brain in my skull. When I get my hands on my little Valkyrie, I'm going to spank the truth from her deceitful lips. She'll be lucky if she can sit down for a week.

Nei, a month.

Just as soon as we rescue her friends and I kill her father.

At least I'll get to deal with that *niðingr*.

"Damrion!" Reaper roars from the back of the warehouse where our communication room is set up. "Eitr is under attack. The Forsaken are at the gates."

"*Faen!*" Damrion and I shout at the same time, racing toward Reaper's location.

I leap over a pallet of wood with Damrion hot on my heels. I dodge another, nearly careening into the doorjamb.

Reaper, Adriel, and Malachi are all crammed into the tiny communication room, a walkie clutched in Adriel's pale hand.

"The call just came through. There are Forsaken at the gates," Malachi says, his tone somber. "The forest is full of *varulv*."

So Rissa didn't kill them all the other night. Gods. How many of the things have the Forsaken made in the last two thousand years? Too many. Far too many, clearly.

"Will the walls hold?" I ask.

"*Ja*. Against the *varulv*," Damrion says. "But against the Forsaken? Not for long."

"We should be there," Adriel growls.

"Abigail sent us here for a reason," Malachi says.

"*Ja*, because she knew this was going to happen, you fool," Adriel snaps at him. "You think she didn't see this? You think she didn't know they were coming?" He spears Malachi with a dark look. "She knew, and she sacrificed herself to save the Valkyrie."

Is that why we're here? Because Abigail was trying to protect Rissa? *Faen*. At this point, I hardly know what to believe. But we're here for a reason, I do believe that. And whatever that reason is, Rissa is at the heart of it.

The Forsaken want her. Abigail knew it. Perhaps even sacrificed herself to keep it from happening. Which means my mission is unchanged. I'll do whatever I must to ensure my Valkyrie survives.

"We have a problem of our own," I say quietly. "There are dozens of Forsaken holding Rissa's coworkers and her father. Unless we free them, they'll be dead by morning."

"Eitr should be our priority, not three humans," Adriel says.

"Not to sound heartless, but he's not wrong," Reaper mutters.

"Abigail was clear. If Rissa's friends die, the world will fall to the Dark," Malachi argues.

"So you just want to let your own people die in their place?"

"I didn't say that!" Malachi growls at Reaper.

"Enough!" Damrion roars, slamming his hand down on the table. "That's enough! We're not leaving anyone to die. Abigail sent us with clear instructions. We're going to do what we came here to do. Everyone else, we send back to defend Eitr. As soon as we're done here, we return to Eitr."

"And if we're too late?" Adriel asks. "If they've already taken her? What then, Damrion? What's your big plan if she's already gone?"

Pure murder flashes in Damrion's gold eyes as he admits for the first time, perhaps even to himself, just how deeply his emotions for Abigail run. "Then Gods have mercy on every Forsaken I come across, for I'll have none."

Adriel grunts, some curious mix of love and pain swirling through his expression, but says nothing further.

I leave them to figure out a plan and head upstairs to fill Rissa in on what's happening. I don't relish telling her any of this. There isn't a single piece that won't break her heart. She's as fierce as a storm and still as gentle as a warm rain, so worried about everyone else. Always, she worries about everyone else.

Everything she feared has come to pass, and I can't protect her or her heart from any of it. All I can do is fight, turning my rage on her enemies. She's her own weapon, but I'm another blade in her arsenal, one designed specifically for war. I can't stop what's coming. But I can kill like no other when it arrives.

"Rissa?" I know the moment I step into our room that she isn't inside. It's cold in a way it never is when she's near. I still check anyway, peering into the bathroom to ensure she isn't showering.

Satisfied she isn't inside, I step back out into the hall, checking each room. Worry flickers to life, quickly growing to alarm. I undo the mask Damrion asked me to place on the bond to keep her from sensing my emotions...and alarm grows to outright terror.

Wherever she is, she's shut me out. I still sense her, but I feel nothing from her, not a single drop of emotion flows through the bond. It's as if she's cut herself off from everything.

"Rissa!" I shout, racing through the warehouse at full speed. "Rissa!"

Fifteen minutes later, we've checked every inch of the warehouse. She isn't inside. The other Fae warriors, along with Stephan and Garrison, check the perimeter and surrounding area, but find nothing. Gods alive. She isn't here.

"She heard us," I whisper, scrubbing my hands down my face. "She heard what we were saying, and she ran." But where? To Eitr to try to save Abigail? To her father's to try to save him and her friends?

Gods. Why didn't she tell me about her father?

"Where would she go?" Reaper asks.

I stare at him, unsure how to answer that question. Unsure what she would have done. She wants to save everyone. It weighs heavily on her.

"She was upset about Abigail the other day."

"*Ja*. But there's a reason she lied to you about her father, Dax," Damrion says quietly. "Why would she?"

"He tried to murder her when she was a little girl."

"We know that." Malachi shrugs when I look at him. "It was in his record when I went snooping."

"Why did she lie?"

"How should I know?" I growl, pissed that they keep pressing the point. She and I haven't had that conversation yet. She isn't here so I can spank her for lying to me about the sorry son of a... *Faen*. "I threatened to kill him."

Damrion eyes me placidly.

"She lied to protect me," I mutter, the pieces falling into place. Of course. She wants to protect everyone she loves, and she loves me. If she'd told me the truth, I would have hunted him down and ended his miserable life. She may be Valkyrie, but she's still human enough to believe that souls can be damned for such things. She didn't want to risk mine on someone who had already cost her so much and hurt her so deeply. Someone she still loves, even though it shames her.

Ah, Rissa.

The Norns chose well when they chose her for this task. She is everything the realms ever got right.

"So she's at her father's then," Adriel mutters. "Lovely. Three humans and dozens of Forsaken."

"Quit bitching and get ready for war," Damrion snaps. "We have a Valkyrie to save."

Chapter Twelve

Rissa

I HAVEN'T BEEN HOME since the night my father tried to kill me, but it hasn't changed much. It's still the same two-story red brick house that gave me nightmares for so long. Only it's older and more worn down now. I don't understand how he lives here, but I've never tried to understand. There's nothing about him I want to understand.

Part of me may cling to love for him, but the rest of me fell to apathy for him long, long ago. I no longer fear him. I no longer hate him. Most of me simply feels...nothing for him.

I see none of the Forsaken Damrion warned Dax about as I slowly approach the house, but I know they're here. I feel them watching me like predators stalking prey from the underbrush. I grip my *ímun-laukr* tight, the biggest part of my consciousness hovering in the well that houses my Light. I don't grab it yet, but I'm ready.

My feet crunch on the gravel as I climb the steps to the front door. It seems fitting that we should do this here, in the same place where my nightmares began so long ago. In the place where my mom read those bedtime stories to me. I never thought they'd turn out to be more reality than myth or that they'd still be playing out all around me, but it feels fitting that this ends where it began.

I'm not stupid enough to waltz inside, though. If they're going to move against me, they can do it in broad daylight while the neighbors peek through their curtains.

"You wanted me," I call quietly, speaking to the door...or through the door. I'm not sure. But I'm speaking to whoever makes decisions on the other side. "I'm here."

No one answers. Nothing moves.

"I came alone," I say. "But you know that already. You've been watching me since I made it to this neighborhood."

Still, no answer.

"I came to make a deal with you. But if you'd rather fight instead..." I reach for my Light now, letting it fill me. I know the neighbors can't see it, but the Forsaken can. "I can do the same thing to you that I did to your *varulv*."

The door cracks open. "We don't make deals, Valkyrie," a man says, his face obscured in shadow.

"Well, you're going to want to make this one."

"Come inside."

"No, thanks. You can send Genevieve and Jessa out, though."

"No, thanks," he says, mocking me.

"Then I guess you don't want to hear my deal." I take a step away from the door.

"We'll hear the terms of your deal and then decide if the mortal girls live."

It's not great, but it's something, at least.

"Is my father still alive?"

"He is still breathing. At least for the moment. Your deal, Valkyrie."

He's dying, then. I should feel something, shouldn't I? Sorrow or grief or anger? Part of me loves him still, but not even that part weeps for him. Not even that part mourns for him.

"His soul for my mother's," I blurt.

The Forsaken says nothing.

"You agree to allow me to ferry the souls of the innocent across the Veil, and you can keep the souls of the damned, the souls of monsters like him."

The Forsaken laughs, a rasping sound that freezes my blood. "Why would we give you half of what already belongs to us?"

"Because we both know I'm the one thing you fear," I say, far more confidently than I feel. I've never been more afraid in my life. But I know they're afraid, too. They have just as much to lose as the Light. More, perhaps. The Light has been losing for millennia. And for the first time, the Forsaken have to face the realization that for all their manipulations and despite all the battles they've won, it still might not be enough to save them. They may lose. For the first time in millennia, they aren't the strongest thing in the realms. I am.

And soon, I won't be the only one. There will be others, four more Valkyrie spun out by the prophecy to stand against them.

But Dax was right. I don't have to fight yet. All I have to do right now is survive. I have to keep myself and the people I love alive. And the best way I know how to do that is to find a way to give the Light time to grow. To give us time to find my Valkyrie sisters.

"If you weren't afraid, I never would have made it up these steps. But my power scares the crap out of you. There are hundreds of you, thousands, maybe. But I could wipe you all out, just like I did your *varulv*."

"You could try," the Forsaken says, his face looming into view.

I skip back a step, startled. Either I drank way too much in the bar, or the Forsaken I spoke with was playing with magic, because this man is not a man at all. He's just pale skin and malevolence beneath a black hood. Two glowing yellow eyes whirl in the center of it, but everything else is just skin so pale it's almost translucent. His mouth is misshapen, his nose deformed, as if an artist tried to draw a face and then smeared the ink.

I reach for more Light, pulling it into me. The nimbus around me expands.

The Forsaken hisses and jumps backward before it touches him.

"Come near me again, and I'll burn you and every one of your buddies to ash," I growl. "Either take the deal or don't, but don't play with me. I'm not your toy."

"We want all souls touched by shadow."

"No. You take only the souls of those mired in Darkness, those who have committed heinous crimes and failed to seek redemption." Dax told me those souls spend eternity in Helheim in torment, paying for their crimes. If they're going to pay anyway, they can pay once and be done. And, for once in their existence, their payment can be good for something. It can help stave off the Dark until we find a way to defeat it once and for all.

"Roaming souls are fair game."

"Then the Forsaken aren't to claim a soul until a Valkyrie has been given an opportunity to ferry it across the Veil. If they refuse, so be it."

"And the Fae?"

"Touch the soul of a Fae, and every Forsaken I find will be burned out of existence," I hiss. "The same goes for anyone with Valkyrie blood. They belong to me."

Something moves deeper in the house. Another Forsaken? I'm not sure. With this one blocking the door, it's hard to tell. But they're up to something. I don't think they have any intention of taking this deal.

Crap.

Maybe it is time to fight, after all. I kind of hoped we could avoid that, at least for now. At least for a little while longer. But I can't force them to accept my terms. I can't force them to cooperate. All I can do is try. For the Fae. For Abigail. And for the nameless Valkyrie still yet to be called.

"Any other demands, Valkyrie?"

"Just a few," I say, trying to keep him distracted long enough to figure out what's going on behind him. "Free Genevieve and Jessa and agree to leave the living out of this. Humans have no place in this fight."

"And yet you're so willing to offer up their souls. Including your father's."

"He damned his own soul."

The Forsaken laughs again, that same rasping laugh that makes my soul quiver. God, it's a terrifying, emotionless sound.

I glance over his head again, watching as shadows move back and forth. What are they doing?

"I also want you to leave Abigail and Eitr alone."

"Is that everything?"

"That about covers it," I say reluctantly, still not sure what they're doing in there. But I'm out of time to figure it out. I brace myself for whatever they're about to spring on me, prepared to burn this Forsaken and his friends out of existence.

"Good."

Even though I know it's coming, I'm still caught off guard when he moves, throwing himself to the side. I release a blaze of Light, expecting to see a room full of Forsaken behind him, waiting to grab me.

Instead, the Light flows harmlessly over Genevieve and Jessa as they fly through the door, stumbling on wooden legs. They crash into me, knocking me to the ground. My head cracks against the cement, a burst of pain ripping through me. The girls land on top of me like dead weights, pinning me in place.

The power I was holding slips from my grasp, flowing back into the well in my soul. I rip through the barrier I erected to keep Dax at bay, flinging open the doors of my soul as the Forsaken grab me, dragging me into the house.

The last thing I see is my father, slumped against the floor in a pool of blood.

Chapter Thirteen

Dax

WAVES OF PAIN AND fear hit me out of nowhere, so intense they freeze the blood in my veins.

Rissa. Ah, Gods. Rissa.

"Faster," I growl at Malachi. I want to peel the skin from my bones and howl in rage. My mate, the keeper of my soul, the Valkyrie I love, is in danger, and there isn't a damn thing I can do. I've never felt more helpless. I've never felt more like killing. "Drive faster!"

"I'm already doing ninety, Dax."

"They have her," I groan, raking my hands down my face. "She's hurting!"

I don't have to say anything else. Malachi hits the gas, and the speedometer shoots upward.

I start praying to every God I can name.

Odin, guide her.
Thor, protect her.
Tyr, give her strength.
Please, please, don't let her die.

Chapter Fourteen

Rissa

I come awake with a jolt, my head pounding. I slowly peel my eyes open, only to come face to face with my father's lifeless body. His eyes are open, staring at nothing. Even in death, he looks terrified. Blood pools around him, soaking through his clothing.

A wave of sorrow—the same I couldn't find outside—whispers through me, though I'm unsure if I grieve for him or for what could have been. What should have been had he been different. Judging by the smell of alcohol in the house and the sunken, sickly pallor to his skin, he never gave up the whiskey. Judging by the state of the house, at least what little I can see of it from where I lay, he never gave up the alcohol-fueled rages, either.

He died as he lived, violently. Painfully. Having never once said sorry for everything he took from me. Not just my mom but my childhood and my sense of safety. My trust in people and, for a long time, my belief in love. He took everything and paid far less than I did.

I close my eyes, blocking out the sight of him. I can't think about that now. I have more pressing concerns. Like the fact that I'm in a house full of Forsaken. Dax is going to be so mad at me when he finds me.

If he finds me.

"Do it," one of them whispers. "Before she wakes."

Do what?

"Is the sacrifice prepared?"

"We have his soul."

"Then prepare to open the portal," the Forsaken who spoke to me at the door says.

The portal? What portal? To Valhalla? I desperately want to crack my eyes open again to see what they're doing, but I can't. I can't let them know I'm already awake. But if they're opening the portal to Valhalla, I need to let them do it. It may be the only way back.

I slowly dip into the well, being careful not to draw on the Light inside.

"As soon as it opens, prepare to go through and start collecting souls," the Forsaken from the door says. "As many as you can contain."

Collecting souls? From Valhalla? Why would they need souls from...?

Shock courses through me as realization dawns. They *don't* need souls from Valhalla. They can take those from anywhere. But they need the Bifröst to travel between realms, just like the Gods did. And the Bifröst was destroyed two thousand years ago. The portal in Valhalla was the *only* piece of it left...and they destroyed it three hundred years ago.

They haven't been collecting souls at their whim for the last three hundred years! At least not any that made it to the waiting place just before the Veil. They can't get there without the portal any more than the Fae can get to Valhalla without the portal. They thought they were destroying the Valkyrie when they destroyed the portal, but they failed to consider the broader ramifications.

Without that portal open, most of the souls they wanted so badly when they murdered the Valkyrie were forever out of their reach.

"Get the Valkyrie's blood. Quickly!"

Nope. If that's what they need to open the portal, Helheim will freeze over first. If that's why they wanted me so badly, too bad. I'll find a way to open the portal myself.

Footsteps start across the room toward me.

I reach deeper into the well, preparing to grasp every bit of Light I can contain.

"Fae!" one of the Forsaken hisses. "Outside."

Dax! Oh, God. Dax is here.

"Hold them off! We're almost finished here."

I allow the Light to pour through me in a fiery storm as I scramble upright.

"Shit," the Forsaken closest to me growls, trying to dodge out of my way. I grab his arm, watching as he ignites with a whoosh of sound.

He screams as he burns.

The Forsaken take one look at him burning and scramble like mice. Too bad for them. I feel like hunting today. I reach deeper into the well, pulling every ounce of Light I can hold into me. Just like I did in the forest, I let it pour out of me. It spreads across the room in spiderwebs, jumping from one Forsaken to the next.

The front door bursts open as Dax, Malachi, and Reaper rush in, *lyststål* spinning. They take one look at the Forsaken going up in flames all over the room and jump in to help. Malachi stabs one through the throat. Reaper stabs another through the heart.

Dax takes out two at once, a savage snarl on his face. As soon as they fall, he twirls, moving on to the next.

"Wait!" I cry as he advances on the one who spoke to me at the door. "Leave him alive."

Dax nods his understanding, kicking the demon's feet out from beneath him. He falls to his knees, not attempting to rise.

Between my Light, Malachi, and Reaper, the remaining Forsaken in the house fall within moments, one after the other vaporizing. Two manage to slip out the door. I contemplate sending my Light after them and quickly change my mind. The neighbors might not be able to see it, but I have a feeling they'll definitely be able to see the Forsaken bursting into flames.

"I've got them," Malachi says, ducking out after them.

I let him go, turning on the Forsaken Dax is guarding.

"Valkyrie witch," he spits, as soon as I set my eyes on him.

"Forsaken scum," I retort, laughing. As if his opinion or his insults mean anything. "You were going to use my blood to open the portal. How?"

He says nothing.

Surprise ripples from Dax. And white-hot anger. That pounds through him like a war-hammer, though I'm not sure if he's more angry at me or the Forsaken.

"All those souls that have been roaming for the last three hundred years?" I murmur to him and Reaper. "They can't get to them. Any that made it to the Veil are still there, waiting to be ferried across."

"*Faen*," Reaper breathes. "How?"

"They can't travel to the Veil without a portal made for that purpose. They needed the portal they destroyed. They were just too dumb to realize that until they'd already destroyed it."

"We didn't destroy it," the Forsaken growls.

"*Ja*, you did," Reaper says. "We watched you do it."

"You saw what you wanted to see, Fae. We intended to take the portal. It sealed itself off."

Dax and Reaper share a look.

"The Valkyrie," Dax says.

Reaper nods. "It must have been a failsafe. Once the last Valkyrie fell and the portal fell under attack, it sealed itself off to keep from falling into the wrong hands."

"How do we open it?" I ask the Forsaken again.

"I'll never tell."

"Fine." I pour my Light over him.

Dax and Reaper jump back as he ignites. Unlike the others, he doesn't scream. He barely makes a whimper as he burns to ash.

"What the fuck?" Reaper says, whirling on me. "We needed him!"

"He wasn't going to tell us."

Reaper shoots a look at Dax, who shrugs. "She's right. He wasn't going to tell us."

The beautiful warrior curses up a blue streak before stomping toward the front door. "I'm going to check on the others."

"He's cranky," I whisper as he stomps out of the house.

"I think he wanted to kill that Forsaken. You beat him to it."

"Oh. My bad."

"Come here."

I slowly make my way toward him, afraid of what he's going to say now that we're alone. Now that he knows I lied to him. It seems like the least of my sins at the moment, considering I also snuck out and came here. But it's the one that weighs the most heavily.

I draw to a stop in front of him as his *lyststål* winks out.

"Are you well, *lyseste ljós*?"

"Yes," I whisper.

"Good." He pulls me into his arms, clutching me to his heart. "Then you can explain to me what you thought you were doing. And you can explain it so well that I lose the urge to spank you into next month," he growls against my ear, his voice rumbling like thunder.

I burst into tears, not because he's angry. Not because I'm trying to get out of trouble. But because I feel his fear and pain. I hear them. And they break me wide open.

"I'm so sorry," I sob. "I didn't want you to kill him. But he ended up dead anyway. I...I...I was going to trade his soul for my mom's."

"Gods alive," Dax mutters.

"I thought if I could c-convince them to make a deal, it'd give us more t-time."

"What deal?"

"The souls of the damned in exchange for all the other souls." I press my face to his throat, letting my tears soak into his skin. "I didn't know they were all safe, Dax. I tried to get them to agree to leave Abigail and Eitr and humans alone, too."

"You asked them for these things?"

I hesitate.

"Rissa," he growls, a warning in his tone.

"M-more like demanded."

He growls again, wordlessly this time. Not that I need words to understand the sound. He isn't very happy with me right now.

"I had to try, Dax," I whisper, pulling back to look at him. "You told me that the most important thing I had to do right now was survive, and you were right. But I'm not the only one who has to survive right now. We *all* have to survive. We all have to find a way to live to fight another day. Because this isn't a war we're going to win tomorrow or the next day. We have four more Valkyrie to find. I can't do that alone. I need you. The Light needs you."

"You have us, Rissa." He wipes the tears from my cheeks. "We're your army to command." His expression turns frosty. "But if you ever do something like that again, may the Gods have mercy on you because this Fae will not."

"I can live with that."

"*Ja*, you can. You will." He presses his lips to mine as if sealing a vow. "I refuse to let you die."

"I won't let you die either, Dax." My gaze flickers past him to my dad. "I won't let you blacken your soul, either."

"But you'll risk blackening yours?"

"He was mostly dead when I tried to barter his soul."

"That doesn't make it better, Valkyrie."

"I know," I admit. "But some souls are so black, there is no saving them, Dax. If using his soul to free my mom's lessened the stain on it, then at least he did something right with it."

"Ah, *lyseste ljós*," Dax breathes, pulling me into his arms again. "He already did something right. He helped bring you into this world."

"Are you very mad?"

"At you? *Ja*. Furious."

Tears well in my eyes again, threatening to spill over. "I'm sorry."

"But I'm more angry at myself, *lyseste ljós*."

"What? Why?" I ask, shock funneling through me. "You didn't do anything wrong!"

"I didn't consider the fact that you loved him still," he murmurs, pressing his lips to my forehead. "I allowed you to struggle alone, believing you had to keep this secret from me."

"I didn't want to love him," I admit in a whisper, my gaze flickering in his direction.

"I know, but that's who you are, Valkyrie. You are Light. He hurt you deeply, but still, you loved him. That isn't wrong." Dax brushes his lips across my forehead. "You're allowed to forgive." He exhales a breath. "Forgive me, *lyseste ljós*. I'm prepared to let Valhalla fall forever to protect your life, but I forgot the most important part of guarding a Valkyrie."

"What part?"

"We're meant to protect your heart, too," he whispers, tipping his head down to brush his lips against mine. "That's what it means to love a Valkyrie."

Chapter Fifteen

Rissa

"Dax." I grab his arm, halting him as we walk through the living room, grabbing everything the Forsaken left behind. His brothers are checking the rest of the house, ensuring we leave no traces of what truly happened here. Genevieve and Jessa are already on their way back home. If they remember anything, it'll feel like a fever dream to them.

There's nothing we can do about the fact that they were missing for half a day. Hopefully, work will just assume they opted not to come back, and they won't remember enough of what happened to disagree. Dax already promised to intervene if it looks like they'll be fired.

There's nothing we can do to hide the fact that my dad was murdered. But I have a feeling people won't look too deeply. If any of the neighbors saw me and the police come looking when they discover his body, they won't find me. I'll be in Eitr where I belong.

The town still stands, and Abigail is safe for now. But we're going back as soon as we're finished here to help drive the *varulv* and Forsaken away. They can't have her. I won't let them.

"What is it, Rissa?" Dax asks.

"What is that?"

He glances down, looking at the little glass bottle he nearly stepped on. It looks almost like a vial from a science lab, only ancient. Whatever is inside looks like a thin rope of light twisted around itself.

"*Helvete*," he mutters, bending down to scoop it up, an uneasy look on his face. He holds it out to me. "I believe this is your father's soul, Rissa."

"Oh," I whisper, reaching out to take the small vial from him. It's so tiny, only a few inches long, and barely any bigger around than an ink pen. The soul is even smaller. I'm not sure what I expected, but it isn't this. "W-what should I do with it?"

"It's up to you. You're the only one who can touch it."

"I think the Forsaken were going to use it to open the portal somehow," I murmur.

"Probably. They use souls as if they're made to be fuel."

I start to take the stopper off to free his soul and then hesitate. I tuck it into my pocket instead. "Maybe I'll just hang onto it for a little while. At least until we're sure it won't get stuck wandering earth."

"Whatever you want, *lyseste ljós*." He brings my hand to his lips, brushing a kiss across my knuckles. "Whatever you want."

"You," I say immediately. "I just want you, Dax."

His bright smile soothes my soul and sets it ablaze at the same time. "Then it's a good thing that I'm a very accommodating Fae, isn't it, *lyseste ljós*?" he purrs. "Because I'm already yours."

"I'm yours too, Dax," I whisper, raising up on my toes to press my lips to his. "Forever."

"*Ja*, you are." His lips come down on mine, his kiss healing.

"I love you," I whisper against his lips, somehow happier than I have any right to be. My father is dead, his soul is tucked in my pocket. The Forsaken are still on the loose. Eitr is under attack. We have ninety-nine problems...but my bond with this Fae isn't one of them. Not any longer.

He pulls me closer, his hand sinking into my hair to hold me to him. A groan rumbles against my lips as he deepens the kiss, his need spilling into me from the bond. I shiver, pressing closer. God, I'll never get used to that. I'll never get tired of it either.

"Uh, Damrion?" Malachi shouts from upstairs, breaking us apart just when it starts getting good. "We have a situation!"

Dax and I both turn at the sound of his voice. Dread creeps through me. I'm tired of situations. My life has become nothing but one big situation.

Damrion pokes his head out of the kitchen. "What kind of situation?"

Malachi appears at the top of the stairs, shock written all over his face. "A woman tied up in the bathtub and Reaper not letting anyone close kind of situation," he says. "I think she's Valkyrie."

Dax and Damrion bolt for the stairs at the same time. I run after them, eager to see this situation for myself.

For once, it sounds exactly like the type of situation I can handle.

A Fae warrior bonding a Valkyrie with Forsaken running amok?

Yeah, I might know a thing or two about that.

Author's Note

Dax, Rissa, and the Fae return in Reaper's story, Valkyrie Fate, coming in April!

Valkyrie Bound Series

The Valkyrie are gone. Valhalla lies in ruin. And for three hundred years, the Fae who swore to protect her borders have been trapped on earth with no way back...waiting for the five women destined to restore order to the nine realms. But they never anticipated that the mortal women called to stand against the Dark in the final battle would need the Fae to protect their souls.

One by one, these ancient warriors find themselves soul-bound to one of the five most powerful Valkyries to ever exist. And, one by one, they find their allegiance beginning to shift. If saving the nine realms means losing the women who own their souls, they'll burn it to the ground themselves.

There's just one problem. The Valkyries have a mind of their own, and they're hellbent on saving every soul they can—even if they have to defy the Fae they love to do it. Forged in battle, bound by fate, and driven by love, these fated mates will change the course of history forever—or die trying.

Valkyrie Heart – http://geni.us/ValkyrieHeart

Valkyrie Fate – http://geni.us/ValkyrieFate

Valkyrie Soul – http://geni.us/ValkyrieSoul

Valkyrie Blade – Coming October 2024 – http://geni.us/ValkyrieBlade

Valkyrie Song – Coming January 2025 – http://geni.us/ValkyrieSong

Valkyrie Bound – Coming in 2025

A Bride for the Beast

International award-winning author Nichole Rose and USA Today Bestselling author Fern Fraser have teamed up to take you on a steamy-sweet adventure to a town where nothing is what it seems.

DRAVEN

I've spent my life in darkness, hidden away from the world.

It's where monsters belong after all, isn't it?

But my curvy maid, Dahlia, brings more than just order to my world.

She brings me back to life and makes me want more.

My beastly appearance doesn't scare her. Nothing does.

Except, perhaps, the father she's running from.

But I won't give her up for any man. This beauty is all mine.

DAHLIA

I spent my life fighting my strict father and his outdated opinions about right and wrong.

Accepting a housekeeping job in another state is a way of proving I can stand on my own two feet.

The moment we meet, Draven's tail sweeps me off them and straight into his arms.

I've never met anyone with more heart and humanity than the sexy, blue-haired giant.

In my father's eyes, Draven is a monster, not a man, but I'm determined to prove him wrong.

This Bride is claiming her Beast.

If you enjoy sassy women, over-the-top men (with a little something extra to offer), and steamy-sweet romance, you'll love this short monster romance!

A BRIDE FOR THE BEAST IS OUT NOW.

Follow Nichole

Like free books? Me too! Sign-up for my mailing list at http://authornicholerose.com/newsletter to stay up-to-date on all new releases and for exclusive giveaways and freebies!

Want to connect with me and other readers? Join Nichole Rose's Book Beauties on Facebook!

Grab signed copies of books, book boxes, and more at http://nicholerose.shop.

facebook.com/AuthorNicholeRose/

instagram.com/AuthorNicholeRose

twitter.com/AuthNicholeRose

bookbub.com/authors/nichole-rose

tiktok.com/@authornicholerose

Nichole's Book Beauties

Want to connect with Nichole and other readers? We're building a girl gang! Join Nichole Rose's Book Beauties on Facebook for fun, games, and behind-the-scenes exclusives!

Instalove Book Club

The Instalove Book Club is now in session!

Get the inside scoop from your favorite instalove authors, meet new authors to love, and snag a free book and bonus content from featured authors every month. The Instalove Book Club newsletter goes out once per week!

Join the Club: http://instalovebookclub.com

Also by Nichole Rose

Find links to my books, audiobooks, the suggested reading order, and a downloadable map of how books connect on my website at http://authornicholerose.com!

Her Alpha Series
Her Alpha Daddy Next Door
Her Alpha Boss Undercover
Her Alpha's Secret Baby
Her Alpha Protector
Her Date with an Alpha
Her Alpha: The Complete Series

Her Bride Series
His Future Bride
His Stolen Bride
His Secret Bride

His Curvy Bride
His Captive Bride
His Blushing Bride
His Bride: The Complete Series

Claimed Series
Possessing Liberty
Teaching Rowan
Claiming Caroline
Kissing Kennedy
Claimed: The Complete Series

Love on the Clock Series
Adore You
Hold You
Keep You
Protect You
Love on the Clock: The Complete Series

The Billionaires' Club
The Billionaire's Big Bold Weakness
The Billionaire's Big Bold Wish

The Billionaire's Big Bold Woman
The Billionaire's Big Bold Wonder
The Billionaires' Club: The Complete Series

Playing for Keeps
Cutie Pie
Ice Breaker
Ice Prince
Ice Giant
Cold as Ice
Ice Storm
Playing for Keeps: The Complete Series

Full-Length Titles
Crash into You
Mister Gregory
Fight for You (coming soon)
Kill for You (coming soon)
God of War

The Second Generation
A Blushing Bride for Christmas

Love Bites

Come Undone

Dripping Pearls

Echoes of Forever

His Christmas Miracle

Taken by the Hitman

Wicked Saint

The Ruined Trilogy

Physical Science

Wrecked

Wanton

Wicked

Ruined: The Complete Series

Illicit Love Series

Irresistible

Irrevocable

Irreplaceable

Irredeemable

Destination Romance
Romancing the Cowboy
Beach House Beauty
Pretty Little Mess
Hitched to the Heartthrob

Standalone Titles
A Touch of Summer
Black Velvet
His Secret Obsession
Dirty Boy
Naughty Little Elf
Tempted by December
Devil's Deceit
A Hero for Her
Dear Mr. Dad Bod
Piped Down

Easy on Me
Easy Ride

Easy Surrender

One Night with You
Falling Hard
Model Behavior
Learning Curve
Angel Kisses

Carmichael Security Series
Truly Mine
Madly Yours
Deeply Hers

Silver Spoon MC
The Surgeon
The Heir
The Lawyer
The Prodigy
The Bodyguard
Silver Spoon MC Collection: Nichole's Crew

Silver Spoon Falls
Xavier's Kitten

Callum's Hope

Snow's Prince

Aurora's Knight

Silver Spoon Falcons
Leia's Playmaker

Aspen's Defense

Gabbi's Goalie

Silver Spoon After Dark
Bound by Bronx

Coming for Coby

Daddy for Davina

writing with Loni Ree as Loni Nichole
Dillon's Heart

Razor's Flame

Ryker's Reward

Zane's Rebel

Oral Arguments

Grizz's Passion

Garrett's Obsession
The Daddy Claus
Submitting to Slade
Dating the Billionaire

Paranormal & Fantasy Titles
A Bride for the Beast (writing with Fern Fraser)
Beauty's Twisted Tyrant

Valkyrie Bound
Valkyrie Heart
Valkyrie Fate

About Nichole Rose

Three-time award-winning author Nichole Rose writes filthy romance for curvy readers. Her books feature head-strong, sassy women and the alpha males who consume them. From obsessed mafia bosses to over-the-top hockey players to ancient Fae warriors and Daddy Doms, nothing is off-limits.

She is sure to have a steamy story just right for everyone. She fully believes the world is ugly enough without trying to fit falling in love into a one-size-fits-all box.

Nichole also writes dark romance as Nichole Fallon.

When not writing, Nichole enjoys fine wine, cute shoes, and everything supernatural. She is happily married to the love of her life and is a proud ringleader in the world's most ridiculous chihuahua circus. She and her husband live in central Arkansas.

You can learn more about Nichole and her books at authornicholerose.com.

facebook.com/AuthorNicholeRose/

instagram.com/AuthorNicholeRose

twitter.com/AuthNicholeRose

bookbub.com/authors/nichole-rose

tiktok.com/@authornicholerose

Made in the USA
Columbia, SC
01 July 2025